Praise for Elizabeth Quinn and Her Previous Lauren Maxwell Mysteries

Lamb to the Slaughter

"Lauren Maxwell shares many of the same qualities of toughness found in Kinsey Millhone and V. I. Warshawski, but at the same time her maternal instincts lend a softness to her character, as well as a fierceness. She is intelligent and resourceful. How on earth did I miss the first two books in this series? It is a situation I will have to remedy soon. . . ."

—Diana Herald, "Books of the Week," *Genreflecting* (online)

"*[Lamb to the Slaughter]* will keep you occupied until bedtime—and beyond. . . . I really liked Elizabeth Quinn's first two Lauren Maxwell books and the third is no exception. . . . Maxwell is a spunky detective."

—*The Pilot* (Southern Pines, SC)

•

"Third in a stellar series. . . . "

—*The Purloined Letter*

•

"An intriguing mystery and a well-evoked setting. . . . The author has an effective narrator in Lauren, and she keeps her story moving smoothly, while sharing her obvious love for Alaska and nature with her readers."

—*The Criminal Record*

Murder Most Grizzly

"The appeal of Alaska as a setting is tremendous, a wild, untamed new frontier with varying cultures and vast panoramas. . . . Highly recommended."

—*I Love a Mystery*

"Intriguing and unusual . . . plenty of suspense [and] sharp dialogue . . . as Lauren . . . learns just how puny a defense a .45-caliber Colt is against an angry *Ursa arctos horribilis.* . . . [She] is an intelligent and feisty female protagonist whose flaws and insecurities only make her character more true-to-life."

—Jane Missett, *The North County Blade-Citizen Preview* (Oceanside, CA)

"A wonderful book . . . Elizabeth Quinn reminds me of Dick Francis in the confident, knowledgeable way that she writes about her subject, with feeling and a wealth of fascinating detail."

—*Tower Books Mystery Newsletter*

"Lauren Maxwell is a detective for our times—an environmentalist, a feminist, and a single mother who balances catching the bad guys with grabbing quality time with her kids."

—Bill Varble, *Mail Tribune* (Medford, OR)

"Exceptional. . . . Absorbing. . . . Quinn makes excellent use of the arctic landscape. With its wild beauty and natural dangers, isolation and cultural diversity, and ecological issues and animal lore, it is proving to be a dramatic setting for crime fiction."

—Gail Pool, *Wilson Public Library Bulletin*

"Readers will . . . get a great deal of enjoyment out of *Murder Most Grizzly.*"

—Kathi Maio, New York *Newsday*

A Wolf in Death's Clothing

"As the story weaves itself through the Alaskan expanse, its rivers and its mountains, its plants and its animals become characters in their own right. . . . Lauren is a likable, plucky heroine."

—Ken Hughes, *Critic's Choice* (America Online)

"Alaska is an incredible place, and this skillful author doesn't let you forget it. The twists that Alaska's vastness works on the minds of the wary and unwary alike is the theme of this . . . second adventure for Lauren Maxwell, recovering widow, mother of two, and pistol-packin' private eye. . . . The solution lies in the clever application of Alaska lore."

—Vince Kohler, *Sunday Oregonian*

Books by Elizabeth Quinn

Killer Whale
Lamb to the Slaughter
A Wolf in Death's Clothing
Murder Most Grizzly

Published by POCKET BOOKS

For orders other than by individual consumers, Pocket Books grants a discount on the purchase of **10 or more** copies of single titles for special markets or premium use. For further details, please write to the Vice-President of Special Markets, Pocket Books, 1633 Broadway, New York, NY 10019-6785, 8th Floor.

For information on how individual consumers can place orders, please write to Mail Order Department, Simon & Schuster Inc., 200 Old Tappan Road, Old Tappan, NJ 07675.

KILLER WHALE

A LAUREN MAXWELL MYSTERY

ELIZABETH QUINN

POCKET BOOKS
New York London Toronto Sydney Tokyo Singapore

An *Original* Publication of POCKET BOOKS

POCKET BOOKS, a division of Simon & Schuster Inc.
1230 Avenue of the Americas, New York, NY 10020

ISBN: 0-671-52770-3

First Pocket Books printing June 1997

10 9 8 7 6 5 4 3 2 1

POCKET and colophon are registered trademarks of Simon & Schuster Inc.

Front cover illustration by Vince Natale

Printed in the U.S.A.

For Nellie
brainy, beautiful, beguiling

Oh, would you seek a cradled cove
and tussle with the topaz sea!

—Robert Service

KILLER WHALE

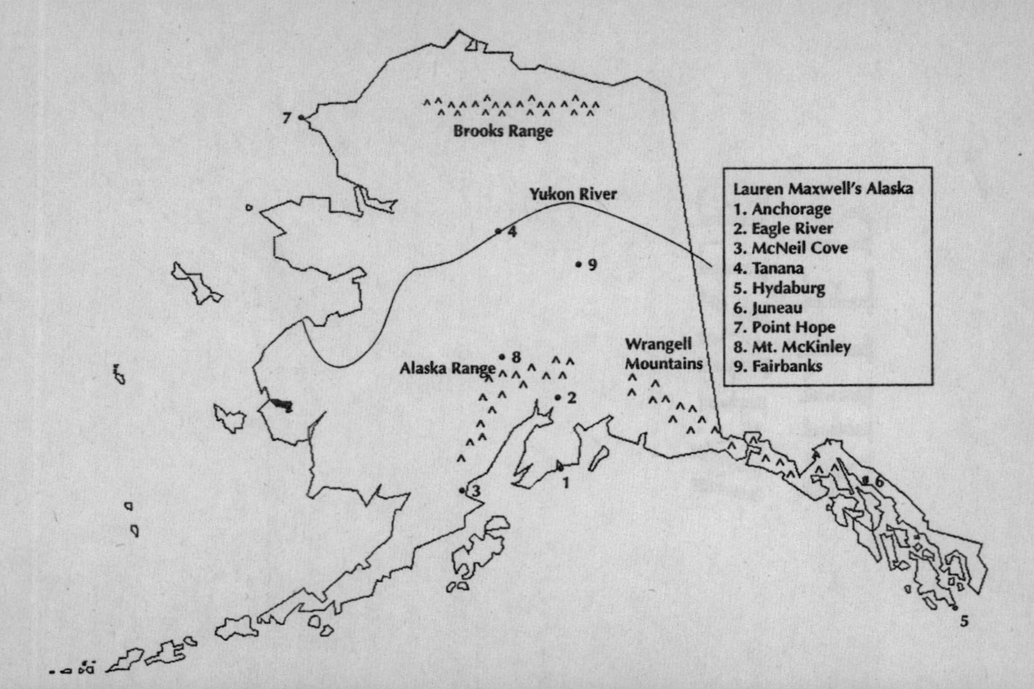
Lauren Maxwell's Alaska
1. Anchorage
2. Eagle River
3. McNeil Cove
4. Tanana
5. Hydaburg
6. Juneau
7. Point Hope
8. Mt. McKinley
9. Fairbanks
Brooks Range
Yukon River
Alaska Range
Wrangell Mountains
1
2
3
4
5
6
7
8
9

1

NOTHING RUINS A FINE SPRING AFTERNOON LIKE a floater. At least that's what my friend, Matt Sheridan, told me when the lengthening days of April warmed the water around Anchorage enough to float the winter's bodies to the surface. A holiday drunk who stumbled into Ship Creek in December, a despairing suicide who dove into a fishing hole on Cheney Lake in January, a hapless adventurer who broke through the ice on Potter Marsh in February—all had wound up in water so cold that, though their deaths were assured, their journeys back to dust had been delayed. But finally came the Alaskan spring, with its oh-so-welcome sunlight, to release the drowned from their unnatural hibernation, allowing the rot to set in that would buoy them back into the world of the living to spoil the fine afternoons of even hardcase cops like Matt. When he made his glum observation over drinks at a lounge on Huffman, right after wrapping up the paperwork on his third floater of the month, I'd nodded and made sympathetic noises, letting my memory of putrefying wildlife kills fill in all the gory details. But I really didn't understand the special horror of a floater, not up close and personal, not then. And when I finally achieved that awful understanding a month later, the knowledge was all the more terrible because my first floater was also someone I knew.

That day dawned gray and misty, as most days do in Hydaburg, a village of about five hundred people on Prince of Wales Island in Alaska's far southeast corner. I'd come to Hydaburg to save the whales. Literally. To save twelve *Orcinus orca,* known popularly as killer whales, creatures beloved by millions around the globe who've seen one in the flesh at an ocean theme park or in the celluloid at a *Free Willy* flick. Saving the whales is part of my job as Alaska investigator for the Wild America Society, the oldest mainline environmental group in the United States. But the purpose of my work in Hydaburg was a lot more complex than simply being part of my job. For me, saving those twelve orcas would be an act of redemption. After all, I was the one who'd sentenced the whales to lifetimes of servitude in water-filled cells. It was all my fault.

As I explained that to Captain Nathan Chaloner on the forecastle of his 110-foot Coast Guard cutter *Kodiak,* the May sun finally broke through the overcast, sending a golden shaft of light to melt the last wisps of mist that clung like gauzy scarves to the low green mountains rising above the waters of Sukkwan Strait. "So, for once, my boss took my advice on pending federal legislation with no questions asked, and look what it got me—twelve captive orcas. I wouldn't blame Boyce Reade if he fired my butt. It's all my fault."

After lowering his binoculars, Captain Chaloner glanced down at me, brown eyes warm in the golden light. "How do you figure?"

"I advised him to sit tight and let the White House work out the particulars of the bill. After all, we enviros aren't exactly popular over there after the way the President's been blasted by our membership and our leadership." I sighed deeply and looked away across the choppy water. "'Let's give him a chance to craft his own proposal,' I said. Who could have predicted he'd engineer a Pyrrhic victory?"

"Exactly." The Coast Guard officer smiled down at me, a wide and winning Hollywood grin, and my heart took a little skip. You don't meet many black men in the southeast; you don't meet many men with looks like Chaloner anywhere. "With all due respect to you, Lauren Maxwell, and to my commander in chief, nobody could have predicted the compromise from hell."

That's what I'd termed this mess in a memo to my boss and the name had stuck. Officially, the mess in question is known as the Marine Mammal Protection Act. First adopted in 1972, the act prohibits live or dead takings of polar bears, sea otters, walruses, dugongs, manatees, whales, porpoises, seals and sea lions in U.S. waters, with exceptions allowed for subsistence hunts by Alaska natives, scientific research and public display. Long before the act came up for renewal, public opinion swayed firmly, and seemingly permanently, against taking more orcas for public display in ocean theme parks. Thank old Willy for that. And although the green's radical fringe disputes the rights of Alaska natives to continue their traditional hunts, most enviros accept the loss of small numbers of marine mammals for the sake of cultural preservation. The real crux of the current renewal fight was the middle exception—scientific research—and my advice to my boss, Boyce Reade, had been to let the White House figure out how to close that loophole. Which the President promptly did. In exchange for a permanent ban—meaning never again—on the taking of marine mammals for scientific research, he agreed to allow the immediate taking of a dozen specimens of each protected species. Sort of a twentieth-century equivalent of Noah's Ark.

As the *Kodiak* cleared the headland of Sukkwan Island, the chop of the strait turned into the swells of Cordova Bay, and I grabbed the rail for support. Chaloner had raised the binoculars to his eyes again and slowly scanned the sea before us for the telltale dorsal fins of the orca pods. After a minute or so, he lowered the glasses and shrugged. "No one in sight."

"No one?" My turn to smile. "You like these orcas, don't you? You think they're special."

Letting the binoculars dangle from the strap around

his neck, he folded his arms and leaned against the rail, his back to the sea. "First time I ever saw an orca was during black cod season when a couple of fishermen complained the whales were stealing their catch. These guys lay out a line each morning, put it down on the sea floor, and then pull it in that night. The rig's about a mile long with a baited hook every yard or so. This pair of fellows said as soon as they started winching in their line, the orcas would show up and gobble the fish right off the hooks."

His eyes went cloudy with memory. "I was just out of the academy and my commander sent me out for a look-see. Sure enough, the winch starts and there comes the pod—thirty-five orcas coming in at seventeen knots, racing in on a foaming wall of water—to clean off every single hook."

His eyes refocused and he flashed me another brilliant smile. "So I suggested a buddy system with two trawlers, one to distract the whales while the other reeled in the catch. And it worked—for about an hour." The smile deepened into a grin. "Then the orcas figured it out, split into two teams, cleaned off the lines of both trawlers, and to show us their appreciation for the new game we'd devised, proceeded to breech and tail-slap and generally raise a ruckus all around the boats."

I couldn't stop my jaw from dropping. "Thirty-five orcas leaping out of the water all at once?"

"Yeah." His eyes glittered as he drawled out that one word. "They're special all right."

I jerked my thumb over my left shoulder. "So I

guess you weren't too surprised when the ecoarmada sailed into the harbor." The President's compromise had attracted forty-plus boats from around the globe to Hydaburg, each crewed by committed enviros determined to stop the whale hunt scheduled to start in the next few weeks. Keeping some semblance of sanity on the sea was Chaloner's job. I cocked an eyebrow in his direction. "But maybe even you were a bit impressed when *Rainbow Warrior* showed up?"

"I'd met the guys from Greenpeace before." He cocked an eyebrow right back at me. "Funny I never met you. Heard of you, of course. Especially after that business up at Denali."

I turned my face into the breeze, letting the salt air wash over me and a moment pass so I could conveniently ignore that last comment. The sun dazzled my eyes. I didn't want to talk about the gunplay at Denali National Park. Or at the Nowitna Wildlife Refuge. Or at the McNeil River grizzly sanctuary. The President might have crafted a compromise from hell but no way could that compare to the hellish summer that fate had fashioned for me the year before. Malice and mayhem, malevolence and murder—things had gone from worrisome straight through wicked and on to wretched in record time. I'd needed months to recover, every month of the fall and winter. Not that time alone had healed me. The endless embrace of love supplied by my kids, Jake and Jessie, had done the heavy lifting in that repair job. Both of them were just weeks shy of their next birthdays—his thirteenth and her ninth—and it seemed like the Maxwell kids had spent the entire year worrying about their mother, who'd metamorphosed from boring old Mom into the latest action hero, over-thirty matron's division. After surviving that terrible summer, I'd stuck pretty close to my home in Eagle River, lapping up all the reviving love my kids could offer. By the time the call to save the orcas arrived, I'd recovered enough to say yes. But I still didn't want to talk about the horrors of the past year.

The shrill scream of the boat's whistle pierced the silence, and I froze, counting six separate blasts. At the first, Captain Chaloner darted toward the gun mounted in the center of the ship and activated the communication box mounted there. "Bridge, forecastle, report."

The reply came on a gust of static. "Object, two niner zero, range one fiver zero."

As the cutter's bow swung onto a new heading, the captain spun back to the rail, raising the binoculars to his eyes. Up on the superstructure, a crewman hoisted a flag slashed on the diagonal, red on top and yellow on the bottom, and a half dozen of his mates exploded from doors beneath the wheelhouse, running toward the motorized raft amidships.

At his spot next to the rail, Captain Chaloner stiffened like a hunting dog on point. I came up beside him. "What is it?"

For the merest second, he paused. "Not sure." He yanked the strap of the binoculars over his head. "Use these. Look for something blue. And don't leave this spot."

He moved toward the back of the cutter, where three crewmen struggled into rubber survival suits while three others lowered the rescue raft into the water. I turned back to the rail, peering through the captain's binoculars in the direction he'd indicated. Way out on the swelling sea, a flash of blue caught my eye and then disappeared. Lifting a hand against the dazzling sun, I studied the green water, waiting for the patch of blue to reappear. There! Somewhere deep in my belly, a little worm of unease began to uncurl as the swelling ocean again raised a patch seemingly torn from the sky—there!

I braced myself with one hand on the rail as the ship bore down on its quarry. Captain Chaloner had climbed the ladder to the bridge. As his ship neared the object, the splash of blue took on definition: spider shape defined as arms and legs, stripe of yellow defined as waistband of a half-inflated buoyancy compensator vest, piece of sky defined as a human in blue scuba gear floating facedown in the cold gulf water. Deep inside, the worm of unease gnawed.

Suddenly the *Kodiak*'s engines growled into reverse, spewing white water as the cutter slowed to a drift. The first crewman in a bright orange survival suit went over the side, dropping into the motor raft and firing up the engine. A second man joined him, kneeling in the bow, and then the raft moved off, seeming to fly across the green swells. The raft approached the floater from the side, the driver holding his position while the man in the bow flipped the diver, slipped an arm around the chest and slowly heaved the floater into the raft, which immediately curled tightly back toward the cutter. The angle obscured my view on their return, but before rescuer and floater vanished from sight, the rescuer's free hand reached inside the diver's hood, searching for the carotid artery, and the gnawing worm deep within me headed for the light.

From my spot at the rail, I watched silently as the cutter's crew hoisted the floater aboard, a pair of men brushing aside rubbery arms to latch on at the armpits while another pair, including the third man garbed in a survival suit, reached for the rag-doll legs. A fifth crewman helped the rescuers secure their raft while his mates gently laid the diver on the deck.

"Too late." The rescuer who'd fished the floater out of the water panted as he crossed the deck to stand above them. "He's dead."

As their commander's steps rang on the ladder from the bridge, one Coast Guardsman raised the diver's head and removed his mask, revealing wide, staring blue eyes, now forever sightless, and skin drained of life, death white as whalebone. "Poor guy." After freeing the hood from under the floater's motionless chin, he tugged it off, revealing blond hair, molten gold in the afternoon sun. "I wonder who he is?"

As I tripped forward, the worm of unease reached the surface, turning my voice into a bleak croak. "He's Sam Houston Larrabee."

2

SAM HOUSTON LARRABEE—HANDSOME, SMART, dead.

I fell to my knees on the deck beside him, reaching for his gloved hand, but someone latched onto my upper arms with a powerful grip and dragged me back. "Give them room to work on him." Captain Chaloner slid his hands to my shoulders for a gentle squeeze of reassurance. "Maybe it's not too late."

The crewmen paired off for the rescue attempt, with a beefy redhead poised stiff-armed over Sam's chest while a slighter sandy-haired man knelt by his head to fill his lungs with secondhand air. He tilted Sam's head to open his air passage and slid a finger into his mouth, scooping out a blood-flecked gob of sputum before sealing his mouth over Sam's still lips. The force of his exhalation lifted Sam's chest.

Captain Chaloner pointed to the bloody smear on

Sam's pale cheek. "Could be an air embolism. Elevate his feet. That may keep the bubbles out of his brain."

Air embolism. The words chilled me. I'd done enough scuba diving to know that catastrophic lung ruptures killed. Lung rupture was the hallmark of a panicked diver, one who'd already run into big trouble. Usually that meant a loss of air which forced an emergency ascent. If a panicked diver held his breath while surfacing, the geometric expansion of the decompressing air in his lungs could rupture the alveoli, the tiny air cells of the lung, and force air bubbles into the bloodstream. One air bubble loose in the brain was all it took to kill a diver.

After ten inflations of Sam's lungs, the beefy redhead rocked forward, letting his weight compress the heart, forcing the blood to flow. Forward and back, forward and back, he rocked to an artificial flub-dub rhythm while the slighter man at Sam's head checked for a pulse in the carotid artery running through his neck. "Blood's moving." He wiped his lips on an upraised arm, leaving another bloody smear. "Steady on—there's a pulse."

A third crewman slid forward to fasten a mask over Sam's face and, with the hissing turn of a dial on a thin blue tank, release pure oxygen to fill his lungs.

The redhead grunted with the effort of his work, and the crewman who'd done mouth-to-mouth squeezed his eyes shut as he felt for the pulse in Sam's neck. After a dozen CPR compressions, the big man rocked back on his heels and paused. "Heart still pumping?"

The sandy-haired crewman snagged his lip with his tooth and then shook his head. "Looks like you're the whole ball game, Red."

Forward and back, forward and back, rocking onto Sam as the cutter rocked on the sea, the hiss of the oxygen tank matched the hiss of the spray tossed up by the bow of the ship as it plowed Cordova Bay on a course for the Sukkwan Strait and Hydaburg. Long after the first beads of sweat appeared on Red's forehead, Captain Chaloner gave the order for one final effort.

After sliding Sam onto a litter, they quick-timed him to sick bay in the bowels of the ship. As I stood in the hatch, leaning against the bulkhead to steady myself against the sea and the horror, they sliced open the top of his wet suit, smeared his chest with jelly, and then Red pressed two paddles against his pale skin. "Clear!" The other crewman fell back as electricity coursed between the paddles, jolting Sam's body in an effort to restart his heart. Once, twice, three times the defibrillator zapped the young man, lifting him floppy-limbed from the table, and three times his heart remained silent and still.

I only became aware of the tears dripping from my chin when Captain Chaloner offered me a crisp white handkerchief and a supporting arm. "Let me take you someplace private, Mrs. Maxwell." He gently drew me away from the sick bay hatch. "Maybe find some coffee."

The sound of our steps stirred up a hollow echo in the narrow passageway. Under my feet, the deck trembled with the vibrations of the cutter's engines, which underscored the sudden silence with a thrumming growl. Dead. Sam Houston Larrabee was really dead. I'd only known him a few days, but in that time he'd made a big impression. When my pal Vanessa Larrabee had heard about my assignment in Hydaburg, she'd insisted I stay with her nephew, a fellow she'd raved about for years. Despite her excessive zeal in praising young Sam's brilliance, I'd been prepared to meet an ordinary young man. After all, childless aunties do get carried away. But Sam Houston Larrabee had actually lived up to his advance billing and had managed to charm me completely in the short time I'd known him, which made his sudden death that much more awful. How could a man who'd been so vital and laughing at breakfast be rendered so hollow and silent before lunch? Just a few hours earlier, those blue eyes had sparkled with mischief when he found me singing along with the radio, belting out "I fall to pieces" when I should have been sectioning our grapefruit.

"Gotcha!" He slowly ambled into his kitchen, ruffling his sleep-tousled blond thatch. "That there's Patsy Cline, and I'm telling."

To distract him from the blush staining my cheeks, I propped both hands on my hips and huffed, "Telling what to whom?"

"To whom? Don't go all hoity-toity on me, Lauren." He cocked his head to one side and stifled a huge yawn. "Telling my cousin Vanessa, that's whom. When she called to ask if you could stay here, she promised me that you were a true daughter of Texas at heart." He pitched his voice higher. "'Lauren likes to pretend she's something special from back East, but don't you be fooled, Sam Houston. She's a good old girl.'" He lifted his arms into a luxurious stretch and tossed me a lazy smile. "That's what Vanessa said. Looks like it's true. Not too many folks back East can sing Patsy Cline these days."

Vanessa. Panic struck me with the force of a blow, and I stumbled. Captain Chaloner caught and steadied me, and then he pushed open a hatch and ushered me inside a deserted wardroom, settling me on the bench of a built-in booth. After promising to return with coffee, he hustled away, closing the door behind him and leaving me alone to grapple with the horror of my first floater and the panic over Vanessa Larrabee's reaction to Sam's death.

As my fingers traced idle patterns against the smooth white enamel of the table, my mind raced back to Anchorage where my friend, Vanessa, struggled to recapture her joy for living after reluctantly parting from the man she considered *the* love of her life. For five years, Lloyd Dorsey had been the still center at the heart of her universe, the man she'd waited all those years to meet. He started out as just another fling, a free spirit who provoked plenty of thought and fun without threatening to cajole her into domestic bliss. Which turned out to be the problem. About three years into the relationship, Vanessa realized that what she really wanted from Lloyd Dorsey was a permanent commitment. By that time, he had her brainwashed into believing a bunch of "butterflies are free" hoo-hah that went out with the sixties. Meaning none of her sizable circle of friends dared to say a word against Alaska's resident Peter Pan, even after he started seeing—and sleeping with—other women. As the months stretched into years, Vanessa just got sadder and sadder, deflating like a party balloon that once tugged against the restraining ribbon but now lay withered among the crumbs on the floor. Soon after New Year's—a holiday she spent alone while Lloyd partied with an old flame in Hawaii—Vanessa finally found the strength to end the relationship, if not her misery. Since then, all of her buddies had been on an unspoken suicide watch, just in case. Even after five months, she was still awfully blue. And the death of her adored cousin, the young historian she'd put through college and graduate school, could only make things worse.

Panic doesn't really capture my emotion as I sat at the narrow white table inside that Coast Guard cutter, heart pounding and mind racing. Only one word does—*terror.* I didn't even want to think about how Vanessa would react when she learned that Sam Houston Larrabee was dead. And right then and there I made up my mind I wouldn't think about it. In the face of stark, raving terror, I reached one unshakable decision. I would be the one to tell Vanessa about Sam's death. I would get to her first. Before the authorities with their official masks of sorrow and before the press with their gut-wrenching questions, I would get there first. No matter what.

As I made that vow, Captain Chaloner returned, carrying a round tray that bore a squat coffeepot and two heavy white mugs. After setting the tray on the table before me, he dug both hands into the pockets of his coat while I reached to pour. "Cream?" One hand brought forth a half-dozen plastic thimble-sized servings. "Sugar?" The other hand proffered pastel packets of assorted sweeteners, real and no-cal.

I snagged a cream and real sugar. "Thanks." The coffee fixings gave me cover to consider the best way to ask a Coast Guard officer to participate in what some would term dereliction of duty. After all, withholding notification of the death from the next of kin wouldn't do much for the service's public relations or the officer's career aspirations. But maybe withhold wasn't the right word. Delay. That was more like it. I didn't plan to ask Captain Chaloner to withhold notification. I planned to ask him to delay notification. And for a very good cause. After I told Vanessa, she'd make sure that Sam Houston's mother heard the bad news from a family member. Wasn't that a worthy cause? Wasn't sparing the grieving mother an impersonal phone call from an anonymous official reason enough to delay notification—just for a couple of hours?

Before I could translate those thoughts into words, Captain Chaloner had a few of his own. "Looks like Larrabee was wreck diving. His air hose was torn and his gloves sliced up." His level brown eyes met mine over the rim of his coffee mug. "Way I figure it, his hose got tangled. After working to free himself for a while, he started running short of air. The gloves suggest he maybe got a little frantic and wound up tearing the hose."

He paused long enough for me to insert a question, but when I remained silent, the Coast Guard officer continued. "That meant he had to make a free ascent. Emergency swimming, he probably panicked, held his breath by mistake, and a lung rupture forced air into his bloodstream. Air embolism—we see that a lot, although it's not usually fatal. Sometimes but not usually."

I blinked back tears and busied myself with my coffee, taking small scalding sips to give myself time. Sam Houston Larrabee had panicked. Meaning he'd known pure fright, all alone in the alien underwater world without the one absolute essential of his species—air. Panicked, frenzied, terrified, as my own Max must surely have been when his plane spun wildly toward the earth. To die in fear. For both men, that seemed especially cruel.

I pushed the thought away, forcing myself to focus on those in need, the living, Vanessa. "Captain Chaloner, I have a huge favor to ask of you."

I set my mug on the table. He nodded for me to continue. Did I just imagine the wariness in his eyes? "Sam's cousin is a good friend of mine, and she's in a bad way emotionally. I fear for her when she finds out what happened to him. Vanessa just adored Sam. Lately, he's been the only good thing in her life."

The Coast Guard officer folded his hands on the white enamel table. "What are you asking?"

I looked him in the eye. "Let me be the one to tell her. And let Vanessa tell Sam's mother. As soon as we get to Hydaburg, I'll catch a seaplane to Ketchikan and from there a jet to Anchorage. I can get home in a couple of hours if you'll just give me time."

Nathan Chaloner glanced away for a moment, a slight frown marring his handsome face. When his eyes returned to mine, the frown remained. "You're asking me to delay official notification so you can inform the next of kin in person?"

I nodded, eyes unwavering but insides quivering. What if he said no?

"Here's what's going to happen when the *Kodiak* arrives in Hydaburg." His voice left no room for second opinions. "I will inform my superiors that our search-and-rescue yielded a dead man. I will then inform the authorities in Hydaburg and attempt to ascertain the identity of the victim. When his identity is established, I will attempt to ascertain the name and residence of his next of kin. When I have found his next of kin, I will request a bereavement detail from the nearest Coast Guard station. The duty officer will either take it upon himself to order notification through the Coast Guard or, if the next of kin resides some distance from the station, the duty officer will inform the nearest peace officers and request that they notify the next of kin."

I kept my voice even, almost bland. "And how long do you think all that is going to take?"

Something sparked behind his warm brown eyes. "Long enough."

"Long enough for me to get to Anchorage?"

"Long enough to give you a decent head start." The thrum of the engine changed pitch, and the floor tilted slightly. "Looks like we're coming into Hydaburg. You'll want to go topside."

I spared a moment to flash Captain Chaloner a thank-you smile and then headed for the main deck. The race was on.

3

Inside the tiny office on the Hydaburg docks that handled reservations for scheduled seaplane service, I darted up to the counter and danced from foot to foot. "Got any room on the next plane?"

The young Haida woman at the desk behind the counter smoothed her long dark hair away from her face, setting off a chime from the carved golden bangles on her wrist. "Oh, yes. For you?"

"Yeah." I dug my wallet out of my day pack and tossed a credit card onto the scarred wood. "What time's the flight?"

"Three o'clock." She glanced at the Olympia Beer clock tacked up on the wall. "Not much wait. Less than an hour."

But not a lot less than an hour, which meant I'd have time to dash home to Sam's place to pack an overnight bag. A vision of his empty bungalow rose in my mind, delivering a quick jolt to my heart, but I pushed the memory aside. I couldn't grieve for him now, not if I wanted to make that plane.

As the young woman stood, I nudged the credit card across the counter. "Can you start the paperwork while I run back to the Mission Cottage to get my gear? Name's Lauren Maxwell—it's on the card."

I waited just long enough for her nod of agreement before tearing back out the door and jogging down the pier to dry land. Someone on *Rainbow Warrior* waved, and I lifted a hand, returning the salute. When I passed *Le Mistral,* the whale hunter's ship, I fought the urge to make a different gesture. To keep myself on track, I concentrated on the scene before me, refusing to be distracted by horror at what had just happened or anxiety about what was to come. As in most of the native villages of southeast Alaska, Hydaburg's homes stretched out along the shore, some fronted by totem poles and all facing the water. Many boasted the distinctive geometric paintings of animals in black and red and blue that are the hallmark of Haida art. A Frenchman visiting the Haidas in the 1790s found their artwork a stunning surprise. "Painting everywhere," wrote Etienne Marchand, "everywhere sculpture, among a nation of hunters." Raven, eagle, bear and whale all stared down at me from the Haida houses and totems as I trotted along the deserted street, intent upon my task. Another hour before the kids exploded from the school on the other side of town, and at least that long before the men reappeared from their work on the water or in the woods. Inside the houses, women occupied themselves with a variety of tasks—curing pelts, sewing button blankets and tending gardens. The Haida are an industrious people, a fact that brought them great favor when the white missionaries arrived. Not that meeting the missionaries favor did much good. In 1786, when the first contacts were made, eight thousand Haida lived among the misty islands. One hundred years later, only six hundred remained.

The last of Hydaburg's homes fell behind, but still I trotted. The missionaries might have favored the industrious Haida but not enough to live among them. Sam had made his home in a relic of mission days, a faded white bungalow set apart from the village, around a few bends of the dead end road and fronting a private cove. The exertion of my run left sweat trickling down the back of my neck, but as I banged up the porch stairs, a glance at my watch told me I'd made good time. Ten minutes for packing plus turnaround time would have me back on the dock with five minutes to spare for signing the credit card receipt.

After pausing just long enough to steel myself against cruel memories, I walked through the door, intending to beeline straight across the entry hall to my bedroom. That plan fizzled when I stumbled, landing hard on my knees and elbows. I raised my head to find Mission Cottage a shambles. The backpack that tripped me had spilled from the small hall closet, along with two fishing rods, a couple of coats and an opened tackle box whose hooks and lures spread menacingly across the faded rag rug. In the living room on my right, couch cushions littered the floor, some with cases half-stripped and all unzipped. Drawers tottered in an unsteady tower beside the desk, stacked amidst a pile of legal pads, paper clips, pencils, unused envelopes, stray receipts and pens. And strewn around the entertainment console, videotapes and CDs made giant-sized dominoes.

"What the hell?"

I lifted myself onto all fours and peered through the shadowed doorway of Sam Houston Larrabee's bedroom. A heap of clothing surged from the small closet, every drawer on his narrow dresser gaped open, and the mattress of his double bed listed to the floor.

After scrambling to my feet, I rushed across the hall, into my own room. Same story. The intruder had thoroughly tossed my belongings from closet, dresser and bedside table, and had even dragged my small suitcase out from under the bed. I plunged a hand inside, gratified when my fingers connected with the cool steel of my 9mm automatic. Thank God they'd left the gun! I stuck the weapon, holster and all, into a bureau drawer and reached toward the clothing strewn across the floor. Who had time to be slack-jawed with amazement at yet another American burglary, even if it did occur in a crime-free native village? A quick glance at my watch offered further prodding. I had to MOVE if I wanted to make that plane.

After snatching handfuls of clothing from the random piles which dotted the floor of my room, I bolted into the bathroom and angled my arm into a reverse plow to sweep mascara, moisturizer, contact lens case and other assorted sundries into my flowered makeup kit. I dropped that on top of the clothes in my suitcase and dug through the cloth heaps nearest the closet until I'd matched a pair of Nikes, which I added to the gear I'd already "packed." Flap, zip, and I was out of there—back across the hall, scoop up the day pack and out through the front door. I wasted precious seconds locking the damned thing, although the old saw about the horse and the barn certainly applied. The impulse is totally irrational and totally human.

My return gallop to the Hydaburg docks taxed me far more than the trip out had. Adding fresh weight to an already burdened heart will do that. Having the suitcase slap against my thigh and numb my fingers didn't help any. The engine of the seaplane roared to life just as I reached the start of the pier. The Haida clerk met me at the office door, trading my credit card and a small clipboard with pen and unsigned receipt for my lumpy suitcase before leading me toward the plane. She handed the suitcase to the pilot waiting impatiently by the open cargo door, tore my copy off the signed receipt that I returned to her and held my day pack while I climbed into the plane. Two other passengers, an elderly native couple, flashed shy smiles as I fell into a seat behind them, buckling my seat belt and pulling it tight. The pilot swung himself aboard, secured the door and took the controls. Within three minutes, he had the plane skipping across the water, straining to become airborne. After that last exquisite moment before friction is overcome, the seaplane sailed free and the scatter of buildings that is Hydaburg fell away behind us.

As the crow flies, Hydaburg is about fifty miles from Ketchikan—over the three-thousand-foot mountains ranging down the east side of Prince of Wales Island, across the inside passage's Clarence Strait, locate triangular Gravina Island, and there you are. For the first part of the trip, the island stretched below us, thickly carpeted with a green shag of trees that had been shaved here and there by clearcuts. I stared down at the checkerboards of destruction, reminded again of the chaos I'd left behind at Mission Cottage. How often did burglars pass up a television, VCR and CD stereo system so prominently displayed in the living room? Why overlook the .35 millimeter camera I'd left atop the bureau in my bedroom or the laptop computer tucked in the corner in plain sight? They'd found my suitcase—they must have found the gun, too. And what about Sam's new Pentium? I hadn't actually seen that it still remained on the desk behind the opened door of his room, but I clearly recalled the ratcheting grind of the hard drive as I paused on all fours, not five feet away. Oh, God, I'd left the computer running! Meaning Sam, too, had left his house with the machine still on. Which was not like him. For all his boyish and devil-may-care charm, Sam Houston Larrabee showed meticulous habits with his historical research, his high-tech gadgetry and his outdoor gear.

The water of the inside passage shone blue below

us. Away to the north, a ferry chugged across the strait, probably heading for Hollis. For a moment, I searched the surface for the triangular shapes of orca dorsal fins. From the air, females are hard to spot because their dorsals rarely exceed three feet, but the biggest males boast fins up to eight feet. Fins of that length are hard to miss from a low-flying plane for anyone who knows where to look. But for the second time that day, the orcas eluded me, hiding somewhere beneath that sparkling surface or holed up in some secluded cove.

Not long after, the plane banked gently, and for a moment, the blue of the sky met the blue of the water, two habitats inhospitable to man blending into a fusion of beauty. What is it about our species that seeks to enter those dangerous beauties? Since the beginning of recorded history, humans have dreamed of flight, and I have no doubt that our Paleolithic ancestors envied birds, too. Surely those ancestors also tested the waters, learned to paddle on the surface like geese, and to hold breath and fin into the depths like fish. But mastering alien habitats is not unique to our species. In fact, who can claim that man has mastered the waters when other air breathers—the dolphins and the whales—need no elaborate machines to survive beneath the surface? And for all their intricacies, our machines do not ensure human survival. My husband's flying machine had carried him to his death, and Sam Houston Larrabee's diving machines had failed him as well.

My stop in Ketchikan lasted only long enough for me to transfer from the seaplane to an Alaska Airlines jet bound for Anchorage with a stop in Juneau. On my way to my seat, I asked the flight attendant if there'd be time for me to deplane in Juneau long enough to make a phone call.

"Not if you're continuing on to Anchorage." He inclined his head toward the rear of the plane. "Once the captain turns off the seat belt sign, you can make a call from the pay phone in the back of the seat in front of you."

About fifteen minutes later, I dragged my credit card through the slit that read the magnetic strip and dialed Nina Alexeyev at the veterinary clinic. A few feet away, the flight attendant finished restocking his drinks cart and wheeled it into the aisle, rattling and clinking toward the front of the plane. On the other end of the phone, Nina's receptionist, Dave, picked up, his flustered voice signaling another hectic day in puppy land. When I explained where I was calling from, he put me straight through to Nina.

"Why are you calling from a plane?" Her voice held no hint of frenzy or alarm. "I thought you were in Hydaburg at least through next week."

As succinctly as possible, I filled Nina in about Sam's death, my fears about Vanessa's reaction and my plan to break it to her gently. "She'll probably have left work before I get there, so I was hoping that somebody could meet me on the Anchorage end so I won't have to chase around town in a taxi looking for her." I stifled a sigh at this further complication. Nina couldn't very well leave the clinic on a rush day. "I guess I'll just rent a car."

"Nonsense. You'll do no such thing. I'll be there with the 4-Runner. What time do you get in?"

When Nina says nonsense, the matter is closed. She's very gentle and also very firm. Kind of like a boulder—she doesn't budge. When Max brought her into his clinic as a partner, I'd objected because Nina is gay. Put it down as irrational fear of lesbians. I was practically raised on it. Most of us were. Fortunately, Max called me on my prejudice and hired her anyway. Their working relationship blossomed into deep friendship, and Nina became a beloved Alaska auntie to my kids. Only dopey old Lauren resisted succumbing to her many fine qualities. Nina's intelligence, kindness, courage, loyalty and other qualities *ad nauseam* failed to thaw the chill between us. Until the stormy day that Max's plane went down. While I became a one-woman search central, Nina stepped in to keep my household going—meals got cooked, laundry got washed and kids got hugged. When my grief took me on a short detour through a bottle, she stayed the course. And later, when I tried to thank her, she pooh-poohed her heroic rescue of me and my family, asking only that she still be allowed to see the kids who were the closest she'd ever get to having children of her own. I not only agreed, I asked her to help me raise them. Within six months, we'd built her a three-room addition to my house in Eagle River, and since then she's kept the fire burning on my hearth when Wild America business calls me out of town. I absolutely couldn't manage without her.

I grinned into the mouthpiece of the telephone. "Hey, gal, you don't have to do this."

Her chuckle tickled my ear. "I sure do, Lauren. That's what friends are for."

Max used to advise me to trust Nina. Learning to accept that advice inflicted one of the harshest lessons I will ever have to endure, but finally I had learned. Trust Nina? I certainly do. In all things.

4

NOTHING LIKE ARRIVING AT THE HOME AIRPORT to find your car waiting right outside the door. Trust Nina, indeed! When she spotted me through the sliding glass doors, she hopped out of the 4-Runner, scooted around the hood and climbed into the passenger's seat. Without bothering to check if she'd lowered the back window—*Of course she had!*—I tossed in my suitcase and slid behind the wheel, adjusting seat and mirrors as I thanked her for playing taxi cab. I eyed the stethoscope peeking out of the pocket of her lab coat and the pen sticking out of the blond bun at the back of her head. "Back to work?"

"Do you have time?"

I glanced at my watch. A bit less than two hours since I'd left Hydaburg meant the Coast Guard had already had a three-hour head start. But most of Texas followed Central Time, putting the hill country around San Antonio three hours ahead of Alaska, into early evening, which could make finding a bereavement detail somewhat more difficult. "I've got time."

While I threaded the 4-Runner through the airport traffic, heading for the Glenn Highway to Eagle River, Nina offered her condolences and then quizzed me about Sam Houston Larrabee's death, taking my emotional pulse. Down low, the radio played softly, tuned to Alaska Public Radio with its chorus of reasonable voices. All at once I longed for heavy metal, for head-banger music to protect me from Nina's gentle and painful questions. Not quite sure that I could hold it all together, I tried for a safer subject. "Kids are at soccer until six-thirty, right?"

"Right." She nodded slowly and looked out the window, studying the flow of traffic on Fifth Avenue, her voice carefully neutral. "Did you get my E-mail about Jess?"

Jess? Clong! Her question ground the gears of my heart. "What about Jess?"

Nina reached over to give my shoulder a quick pat. "She's okay, Lauren. I'm just a little worried about her. About her soccer, really." She sighed heavily and looked away. "I wish you'd gotten my message."

After downshifting to third, I swung the 4-Runner onto the ramp for the Glenn Highway. Our conversation had just moved onto extremely tricky ground, and the next opening gambit would have to come from me. Nina carefully busied herself looking out the window, knowing quite well that my generosity with my kids only went so far. I certainly did trust her in all things. Or just about. But every once in a while the grizzly bear mother inside of me asserted herself, baring three-inch claws for a quick swipe in Nina's direction. At my worst, I figured that such unpredictable flare-ups meant that cheap and convenient babysitting summed up the real reason I'd invited her into our home. At my best, I recognized that my wrath resulted from unresolved grief that my children's father couldn't share in important decisions about their lives.

A three-point glance—rearview mirror, side mirror, blind spot—and then I eased the 4-Runner onto the highway, letting a quiet cleansing breath escape between my lips. What was the worst Nina could tell me? That Jess got a red card and was tossed from the last game? That the skills of her teammates had finally caught up to my little jock? "So why don't you tell me about Jess's soccer? What's got you worried?"

Nina shot me a quick look and folded her arms across her belly. "None of those girls is having any fun. Nobody laughs. Nobody even smiles. They smirk. From what I can see, practice consists of bitch-bitch-bitch interspersed with a couple of drills. Scrimmages remind me of a fox hunt—the first kid who screws up gets hounded to death by the rest of the team."

Heat rushed to my cheeks. "Jessie's picking on kids who make mistakes?"

"Not Jessie. She's the only one who doesn't." A bitter smile twisted her lips. "At least not at practice.

She saves up all of her carping for the family. At dinner, we get to relive every unpleasant moment."

Unpleasant wasn't a word I associated much with Jess or with soccer. I'd played a little bit in high school, way back in the dark days before federal law required equal access to sports for girls, but Jake really introduced the Maxwell family to the game. My megawatt son just keeps going and going and going, and that talent for endurance proved perfectly suited to a game that consists of two forty-minute halves with no time-outs.

As we came up on milepost thirteen, I took the Eagle River exit and swung onto the old Glenn Highway, heading toward the veterinary clinic. When Jessie started playing, her greatest talent proved to be her intelligence. While other kids ran around without a clue, their parents screaming *Kick it! Kick it!* my little girl resembled William Tecumseh Sherman on his march to the sea—organized, determined and relentless. Talk about the big picture! Right from the start, Jessie could see the whole field and understood the fundamental strategy of the game. Which was why last fall I'd allowed myself to be talked into letting her join a specially selected team destined to play a more competitive brand of soccer. As soon-to-be nine-year-olds, Jessie and her teammates practiced four nights a week and traveled to out-of-town tournaments every other weekend. Although she'd never said anything, I'd long suspected that Nina did not approve. Seemed like my housemate made sure I saw the sports page whenever a new horror story broke about an abusive tennis dad or vituperative skating mom. And although I didn't like to admit it, my daughter's current soccer gig might owe less to Jessie's love for the game than to my own pride in her kick-butt performance.

I turned into the gravel parking lot of the clinic, pulling up in front of the door. "Sounds like I better get to that tournament in Juneau."

Nina swung open the door and got out. "All the way from Hydaburg? Can you manage it?"

For a moment, a vision of my next VISA bill floated through my mind, a page blackened with the dense type of endless transactions. I blinked before my mind's eye reached the bottom line. "Gotta do what I gotta do."

With a satisfied nod, Nina swung the door shut. As I eased up the clutch, she mouthed words through the grimy glass—*Tell Vanessa I'm so sorry*—reminding me again of the real reason for my quick trip home.

Fortunately, Vanessa lived at the northeast end of Anchorage, in a town house near Centennial Park, which spared me from returning to the city. If she was home. After retracing my route back down the Glenn Highway, I took the turnoff nearest her house and cruised slowly through the parking lot. Spotting the red Trans Am in her carport, I parked the 4-Runner, detouring past Vanessa's car to feel the still-warm hood before taking the concrete walk that led to her front door. I spared one glance for the large, freshly planted terra-cotta pot at her entry and then jabbed a finger against the doorbell.

"Comin'!" Even muffled by the wooden door, her twang sounded like something out of a well, which probably meant she'd gone upstairs to change. The rapid *bump-thump* as she skipped down the stairs proved me correct. *Sshhhtt*—the chain lock slid free. That's Vanessa all over. The only Alaskan I know who's really earthquake-prepared, but she opens her door to anyone who knocks. *Snick*—the dead bolt retracted. And there she was—wide, ready smile under a big cloud of red hair that fell to the gold silk shoulders of her lounging pajamas.

"Why, sugar—" Her glance moved past me to the empty sidewalk beyond. Vanessa's smile faltered as she stepped aside, ushering me into her town house, and the color drained from her cheeks. "What are you doin' in town? Is Sam—"

Break it to her gently? Who was I kidding? With one smooth motion, I reached out with both hands to grasp hers. "Sam's dead, Vanessa. He died this afternoon."

Her face crumpled, and she sagged against me. "Oh, God!"

The anguish in her voice freed the tears I'd swallowed all afternoon. I slid my arms around her trembling shoulders and finally allowed myself to cry. Since Max died, each loss feels like losing him all over again, but Sam's death hurt the most. He was all the things my husband had been—too young, too vibrant, too promising—and the fact that he'd lived life fully only made his life's sudden end even harder to bear. All of my anguish—for Max and for Sam—

spilled out of me, streaking down my face to soak the silk covering Vanessa's shoulder. After the storm of tears finally subsided, I left one arm around her shoulders, holding her erect, and steered my sobbing and shuddering friend to the white leather couch in the living room at the end of the entrance hall. When I lowered her to the cushions, she slumped against the armrest, her floppy and lifeless limbs providing me with an unintentional reminder of Sam's failed rescue.

Forcing that memory out of my mind, I sat down beside her and took her hand, squeezing firmly. "We have to let the rest of his family know. They should hear it from us. From you."

Vanessa groaned, pummeling me with a sick and desperate moan, and turned her face into the cushion.

I squeezed her hand again, keeping a steady pressure. "Vanessa. We've got to. Don't make them go through what I did. Don't leave them to the stranger who knocks on their door."

For a long moment, she didn't move. Then she visibly gathered herself, meeting my squeeze with a firmness all her own, and heaved herself upright. I steeled myself for her questions, but she asked none. Instead, she blotted her eyes with fisted hands, smearing mascara across her cheeks, and tossed me a grim nod. "You're right, sugar. I guess I owe them that."

I followed her into the kitchen, hiking a hip onto the other stool at her counter while she sank into a seat and picked up the phone. She punched in a string of numbers, identified herself to whoever answered and asked for Mr. Jesperson. A three-beat pause and then her eyes filled with tears. "I'm calling because Sam Houston Larrabee is dead, Jimmy. Will you go on over and tell his mama?"

Emotion speaks without words, and though I couldn't hear exactly what Jimmy Jesperson said, his surprise and sorrow came to me quite clearly from the earpiece of the phone Vanessa held out to me. "Tell him everything, sugar." She choked back a sob. "I just can't."

"Mr. Jesperson?" I tucked the phone between my ear and my chin. "This is Lauren Maxwell, a friend of Vanessa's. She asked me to take the phone now. To answer any questions."

Jimmy Jesperson asked tons of questions, firing off a fusillade in his soft, Southern drawl, so many questions posed so carefully that when I later discovered him to be a lawyer, I awarded myself a dunce cap for not having already figured that out. As I answered Jimmy's questions, Vanessa folded her arms on her kitchen counter and rested her cheek against them, face turned away from me. Quickly but thoroughly, Jimmy guided me back through my day, collecting the when, where and how of Sam's death and reprising the information I'd gathered from the Coast Guard. Once or twice he excused himself, and though the words came to me somewhat muffled, as though he'd rested the phone facedown upon his desk, I overheard the fusillade of orders he fired at the Texas end of the connection—*check with the Coast Guard, call the airlines, get in touch with the funeral home, have my car brought around*—before he had some for me.

"Beg pardon, Mrs. Maxwell. You still there?"

"Yes, sir." I had a sudden urge to stand up and salute, and not just because he got the name right after only hearing it once.

"All right, then. I want you to get yourselves out to the airport. Tickets will be there for you, and I'll have a car waiting in San Antonio."

"You're expecting me in Texas?"

His voice remained smooth as silk, unhurried and unruffled. "Why, yes. I don't expect Vanessa's in any shape to make the trip alone."

I glanced down at my friend. In the time I'd been talking to Jimmy Jesperson, she hadn't moved. Except for her shoulders, which vibrated now and then with a deep shudder that reminded me of my Jess at her most helpless. "You're right. She isn't."

He didn't thank me. Not then. And he didn't have to. After all, that's what friends are for.

For the next two days, I played Vanessa's shadow, staying close as she threaded her way through the jammed viewing room of an East Texas funeral home and trading solemn glances across the raw and gaping hole of Sam's grave as the minister called down blessings while the coffin sank from view. *". . . for dust thou art, and unto dust shalt thou return . . ."* At those words, a chorus of wounded moans rose from the family chairs beside the grave. Among those groans was Vanessa's, and I moved into position near her chair, ready once more to bear a portion of her burden of pain and sorrow. My friend had managed to hold herself together as family and friends tossed clods of earth into Sam's grave. To the uninitiated, the burial seems the worst part of death, the hardest part of the ritual, but in a day or a week or a month, most mourners learn the truth. That's when they grab the telephone and punch in the number, blissfully forgetful until the disconnect message reminds them that there will be no more phone calls. Too often the call that does come is an innocent reminder—late library books, photos awaiting pickup, dry-cleaning past due. Losing Max had taught me that there are endless worst parts and infinite hardest parts in every death.

In the limousine, on the way back from the cemetery, Vanessa suddenly reached for my hands, squeezing hard. "I'm coming with you to Prince of Wales Island. I'll see to his things. I can do that much. I can't bring Sam back, but I can spare his mama that."

I stiffened. "But what about your life? Your job?"

Her eyes glittered with tears. "What life? I'll use my vacation. Maybe take a leave of absence." A single tear streaked down her cheek. "Or I can quit. It has to be done. Somebody has to organize Sam's papers, pack up his house, settle his affairs."

Pack up his house? At those words, my mind flashed an instant replay of Mission Cottage with the tumble of belongings spilling out of every closet. Pick up Sam's house sounded more like it. And why would a burglar overlook the television and VCR, the CD player and the computer, and my 9mm, for God's sake?

She tightened her grip on my hands. "Don't you see? I made him love Alaska. I kept after him. Letters, books, photographs—I swamped him. I wouldn't leave him alone. I taught him to love Alaska, and so he came north. Now he's dead. And it's all my fault."

She dropped my hands and blotted her eyes with her fingers. "I'm coming with you, Lauren. Please don't try to talk me out of it."

Great. Just what I needed—another problem requiring my immediate attention. First there were the dozen orcas with their freedom on the line. Then there was my Jessie with her childhood on the line. And now there was Vanessa with her sanity on the line. Bing, bam, boom—one damned problem for every role I play. But, after all, that's what ecowarriors/mothers/friends are for.

5

To get back to Hydaburg, Vanessa and I took the scenic route, opting to travel up the inland passage, ferrying over the Alaska Marine Highway from Bellingham, Washington, back to Prince of Wales Island via Ketchikan and Hollis. Vanessa spent most of the forty-hour trip to Ketchikan sleeping in the two-berth cabin we shared belowdecks. I spent most of my waking hours on a sentimental journey, moving between the deck and solarium to study the water and mountains we passed and relive my first trip up the inland passage when Max originally brought me to the Great Land.

Alaska was his idea, not mine, and I'd made it clear that I considered our move nothing more than a tryout and definitely not permanent. Max indulged my fantasy, as he would indulge me in so much, even as he mounted his campaign of persuasion. The ferry represented the first salvo because he knew how much I loved the ocean. When we were falling in love at Berkeley, we spent our free weekends hiking the forested slopes at Big Sur, mesmerized by the surf-tearing rocks at Point Lobos, or baking on the sands north of Santa Cruz. To most people, Alaska conjures up visions of ice, but the Great Land is born of river and sea. Max used my passion to bend my will to his way, making my first visit to Alaska the culmination of a leisurely cruise among dazzling green-greener-greenest islands with wild, storm-tossed shores where seals adorned the rocks, orcas frolicked the waters and eagles soared the skies. He pitched our tent on the deck, making sure to leave off the rainfly so I could see the stars overhead, and we slept in the clean, crisp air, lulled by the gentle sway of the sea. In those days, many Alaskans still preferred the relaxed ambiance of the ferry to the hectic speed of air travel, so we met a scruffy bush miner who regaled us with dreams of gold, a weary Tlingit dance ensemble who detailed the superior comforts of subsistence life and an earnest white native who explained why the Last Frontier required little improvement from Outside. All were warm, friendly and absolutely enamored of Alaska. By the time the ferry reached Haines, so was I.

On the final leg of that first journey, we traveled overland from Haines, through Porcupine and Destruction Bay with the St. Elias Range to our southwest and the Dawson Range to our northeast, until we made the turn at Tok to cut south through the Mentasta Pass of the Alaska Range and on into

Anchorage. Vanessa and I would also finish our trip on land. Before the ferry left Bellingham, I'd called a friend of Sam's in Hydaburg. Owen Stuart promised to leave Sam's battered old Toyota Land Cruiser—the small, rugged, 1970s version, not today's to-die-for glitzmobile—in Hollis with the key in the ashtray so we could drive the thirty-six miles back to Hydaburg, a shorter trip between smaller mountains but overland just the same.

As the first passengers began to load onto the ferry, I'd also made a call to my boss at the Washington, D.C., headquarters of the Wild America Society. A colleague of mine calls Boyce Reade the thinking woman's beefcake—gorgeous, intelligent and oh-so understanding. On the big stuff and the little stuff, he's never let me down. That day proved to be no exception. When I'd called from Seattle three days earlier and announced I was halfway to Texas, he'd listened to my explanation for my sudden departure from Hydaburg and agreed that I could be spared from the whale watch for a few days. When I called from the ferry terminal in Bellingham and announced my intention to take the slow boat back to Prince of Wales Island, Boyce offered no objection. He's not one of those control freaks who insists on micro managing my work from a distance of six thousand miles. He's one of those rare bosses who actually trusts me to do my job and seldom second-guesses my decisions. Although I'm technically employed forty hours a week, I threw away my time card long ago, by mutual consent. Some weeks I work one hundred ten hours, some weeks I work twenty hours, but I never ask for overtime or pad my expenses. The latter can run rather high, what with chartered planes and Alaska prices, which is one reason I'd camped out with Sam Houston Larrabee for my stay in Hydaburg. Since the United States elected an "environmentalist" president, donations to all conservation charities are way down. Bunking with Sam promised to keep expenses to a minimum for what looked to be a couple of weeks stay. Just exactly how long that stay would be was the first question I asked Boyce.

"Maybe not all that much longer." I detected a frown in his tone of voice. "Looks like the whole thing could be over sooner than we thought."

My heart lurched. "What's happened?"

"Nothing yet. The permits for the orca hunt still haven't been issued, but the roadblock is bureaucratic, not political. The issue has zero visibility with the public. In terms of the media, this story is a non-starter."

I gripped the phone tightly. "That doesn't make any sense. Every kid in America dragged his parents to see *Free Willy,* and what about all that hoopla when they moved that orca from an amusement park in Mexico City to an Oregon aquarium?"

Boyce's chuckle rang bitter in my ear. "That was then; this is now. Our sources in the departments of Interior and Commerce say neither secretary is feeling any heat on this issue, and permits for the taking of twelve killer whales will be forthcoming, probably early next week."

A blade of guilt sliced through me. If I'd stayed on Prince of Wales Island, the story would have flourished! I'd have made sure of that! "But what about all the reporters in Hydaburg? Every third guy in that town is toting a minicam on his shoulder."

"Nobody's gone home yet, but from what I've been told, the journalists on site are mostly stringers who have to fight for column inches and air time to begin with." A touch of disdain entered his voice. "The brand-name reporters are still in D.C. or New York, where the 'big' stories are."

"And too damned bad for the other five-plus billion of us who think there's more to the world than Wall Street and Capitol Hill, right?" The scorn in my voice far outstripped his. "Sorry, Boyce, but network news makes me sick these days. From this distance, the newscasts strike me as boring, safe and utterly clueless. I don't even watch anymore."

"Join the parade. The networks have lost millions of viewers, which is why we're looking at CNN, MTV and alternative media to promote this story." Now his voice came through as all business. "What we need is a hook, something to hang this story on that's more than just 'Save the Whales.'"

"You mean a gimmick?"

"No, not a gimmick. Something real, something authentic. Here's an example. Before Mount Saint Helens erupted, the media went wild for this old man who lived in a lodge on the mountain and refused to evacuate." Enthusiasm built in his voice. "Night after night, as everyone waited for the eruption, there'd be an update on the guy. 'Still refuses to leave,' or 'Vowing to stay till the bitter end.' The old fellow personalized the story, made it real and concrete for people. And when the eruption finally came, the only thing viewers really wanted to know was how the old man made out."

"He didn't." I hated to burst Boyce's balloon, but facts are facts. "His name was Harry Truman, and the blast vaporized him."

"That's right. He died. Tragic." Boyce paused a moment to show proper respect for the dead. "But his death isn't the point. The thing to keep in mind is the way Harry Truman's decision to stay caught the public's attention and made Mount Saint Helens a global story, even before the devastating eruption. That man's dilemma hooked the public's attention, drawing them to the larger story. That's what we need for the orcas—a hook. And that's what I want you to concentrate on finding while you ferry back to Hydaburg. Find us a hook."

Find a hook, bait a hook—I pushed the image of an orca impaled on a nasty curl of steel out of my mind and focused on the rest of Boyce's instructions. When he asked me to keep in touch via E-mail, I had to explain that I'd left my laptop back at Mission Cottage. But I promised to fire up the modem as soon as I reached Hydaburg and send him a message outlining my ideas for hooking public attention on the plight of twelve killer whales facing lifetime imprisonment in concrete-lined pools.

Vanessa finally surfaced not long after the ferry crossed back into American waters, clearing Cape Fox and heading into the Revillagigedo Channel. I stood at the rail admiring a spring-swollen creek that gushed between two tenacious Sitka spruce and spilled down a sheer, granite cliff in a long veil of water edged with a lacework of mist. She came up beside me, snuggling her hands into the pockets of her fleece-lined anorak, and with a quick glance, oriented herself. "Misty Fiords, huh? We're almost there."

I nodded my agreement. "How are you feeling?"

She took a three-count before answering. "Almost human." Then she shot me a quick glance and turned her gaze back to the spectacular scenery of Misty Fiords National Monument. "I never asked . . . what happened . . . or how it happened?"

A squirt of annoyance chilled me, and I shivered. The Why she'd figured out, placing the blame squarely on herself for luring Sam Houston Larrabee to Alaska with her tall tales and her generosity. But contrary to the intellectual discipline ingrained by her scientific training, she'd shrugged past the concrete data on the details of the diving accident. Which offered eloquent testimony of just how much her equilibrium had been thrown by his death.

I took a deep breath and let the air leak out slowly, draining my annoyance with it. After all, when Max disappeared, I'd gone a bit crazy myself. "He was wreck diving. He did it a couple of mornings each week."

Wreck diving? In Cordova Bay? That meant deep water, probably not too many wrecks. And no boat! So how did Sam get out there in the first place?

If Vanessa noticed my momentary pause, she didn't say anything, instead concentrating—hard—on the passing scenery. I continued without a prompt, choosing my words carefully to avoid revealing the inconsistency I'd suddenly discovered. "I just happened to be on the Coast Guard cutter that found him and tried to revive him." I forced down a shudder when a macabre rerun of that awful morning rose in my mind's eye. "Those Coast Guard guys knew what to do, and they did it all. But nothing worked. Sam was gone before they got him out of the water."

Now came the hard part. I took Vanessa's arm, linking mine through hers, as much for my own support as to offer her comfort. "From the looks of it, Sam got tangled in a wreck down there." But *was* there a wreck in the middle of Cordova Bay? "He got free, but not until his air hose had torn. He probably started an emergency ascent and then panicked. He held his breath, which forced an air bubble into his bloodstream."

She turned her face toward mine, eyes bleak but steeled with certainty in the gray morning light. "Sam wouldn't panic. He was too painstaking to panic."

Another squirt of annoyance followed that comment. No one's immune to panic—no one. Yet in the short time I'd known him, Sam Houston Larrabee had indeed struck me as a man who took pains—not methodical but meticulous. The kind of guy who didn't get tangled in underwater wrecks or any of the other pitfalls in life. The kind of guy who remembered to let his air escape on a free ascent and to shut off his computer before leaving his house. In the turmoil of my hasty departure from Hydaburg, I'd overlooked too much. Certainly far more than any burglar would overlook. Two computers, a camera, a CD player and a television? And what about the tackle box spilling out of the hall closet and the clothing spilling out of mine? There's only one difference between a burglary and a search—what gets left behind.

The ferry chugged on through the misty morning, and at the rail beside me, Vanessa waited for my response, eyes welling with fresh tears and arm still linked with mine. All at once, I had nothing I could say to ease her grief, so I simply shrugged and remained silent. But internally the investigator went on alert. Sam's death and the break-in at Mission Cottage had to be related. Meaning somebody wanted Sam dead? But why? And what had he owned that proved more valuable than his life?

I glanced at my watch. Twelve more hours to Hydaburg, and then I'd stop asking questions and start finding answers. The jumbled mess of Mission Cottage was the place to begin, but I had one little problem. Vanessa. The scene at Sam's house would inevitably add to her pain. And my explanation for the mess would only make things worse. Murder always does.

6

Some words stick in the throat. Like *murder.* The more I replayed my mental videotape of the scene at Mission Cottage, the more convinced I became that Sam had been the victim of a search, not a burglary. That conviction added a whole new dimension to his "accident." As a rule, I'm not much of a believer in coincidence, and the intersection of Sam's death and the Mission Cottage break-in struck me as a real whopper of a coincidence. So my thoughts turned to other explanations, including murder. Around the ninth grade I'd gotten over my extrovert's habit of blurting out every thought that entered my mind. But even though I did want to tell Vanessa about my sudden suspicion of the circumstances of Sam's death, even though common sense demanded that I warn her about the mess we'd find at Mission Cottage, I simply couldn't find the words.

Not that I didn't try. For the rest of the day, I tried. As the ferry pulled into the dock at Ketchikan, I decided to wait until after we'd made our connection with the ferry to Hollis. In the middle of Clarence Strait, on the deck of the Hollis ferry, I cleared my throat but got no farther. After Sam's Land Cruiser growled to life beside the dock at Hollis, I figured the engine racket made conversation impossible. And when Vanessa closed her eyes for the thirty-six-mile drive to Hydaburg, I concluded she needed rest more than she needed further bad news. Scaredy-cat, chicken, gutless—I was all of those and worse. By the time I pulled the Land Cruiser into the short driveway at Mission Cottage, I'd concluded that only one course of action remained—faking it! When the door of Sam's house swung open to reveal the chaos within, my jaw would drop with surprise and amazement that would only deepen as we walked from room to room, taking in the enormity of the disturbance. Since Vanessa still hadn't regained her equilibrium, I counted on her to overlook the fact that I'm a terrible actress and only slightly better liar. That was my plan, a desperate scheme for which I am truly ashamed. Thank God I didn't have to use it!

When the door of Sam's house swung open—*from the inside*—the entry hall proved to be orderly and spotless, as did the living room, Sam's bedroom and my guest bedroom. In fact, the only hint of disorder came from the kitchen, where a clatter of pans and hum of conversation suggested a party in progress. After hasty introductions, Vanessa ducked into the bathroom while I turned to Owen Stuart and, using all the strength I could muster, managed to keep my voice down to an accusatory whisper. "What the hell is going on here?"

He took a step backward, and his blunt-fingered hand rose to his gingery beard, which contained lots more hair than the graying monk's tonsure ringing his scalp. "I . . . we . . ." His glance flicked toward the kitchen door, but no one appeared to rescue him, so he squared his shoulders and met the beast head-on. "A few of Sam's friends came by to help me pick up the place. We planned a sort of potluck. A memorial, if you will."

Talk about nerve! Not only had they screwed up the damned evidence, they'd also arranged a damned wake! A blaze of anger pushed my heartbeat into overdrive, and I forced myself to take a mental ten-count to keep from punching Owen Stuart. True, Stuart had befriended Sam the day he arrived in Hydaburg, and Sam had granted him free run of Mission Cottage. They'd made quite a Mutt-and-Jeff pair—the tall blond Texas back-slapper with the friendly grin and the stocky graying whale biologist with the bashful smile—and had bridged differences in age and personality to become fast friends. Which most likely meant that Sam Houston Larrabee's death had left Owen Stuart hurting pretty badly. But, at that moment, I couldn't see past my own rage. Even after a ten-count, venom infused my voice. "I can't imagine why you thought you had the right to clean up this place. I only hope you had the good sense to notify the village public safety office first."

"The public safety officer? Why would I notify him?" He took another step back, and his hand dropped from his beard, joining the other hanging loosely at his side. "Somebody had to clean up, and I was the obvious choice. You *did* ask me to drive the Land Cruiser to Hollis, Mrs. Maxwell." A cajoling note infected his voice. "The computer was on, and I just turned it off. I hope that is all right? I am not very good with technology."

My lip curled as I glanced from the entry to the living room. "Looks like you're a wizard with the vacuum, Owen. I doubt it's even worth calling the cops now. You haven't left a trace. Any idea what he was after?"

"What *who* was after?" A glint of anger invaded his blue eyes, and his voice roughened. "What are you talking about?"

The harsh note in his voice finally penetrated my rage, and for the first time, I considered the situation from Owen Stuart's perspective. Heartsick at the death of his young friend, he'd eagerly agreed to deliver the Land Cruiser to Hollis to make our return to Hydaburg that much easier. When he'd come to pick up the truck, he'd probably found the cottage in shambles and decided to set things to rights. After all, I hadn't mentioned the break-in when I called him. I hadn't even notified the local authorities. And to further ease our return to Sam's empty house, he'd gathered a few friends to reminisce over a potluck supper. From the standpoint of a grieving heart, all of Owen Stuart's actions made perfect sense. After a quick but heartfelt apology, I asked for his explanation of the cottage's disarray.

"Kids, most likely." He spread his hands and shrugged. "Teenage vandals. Every town has them, even Hydaburg. Probably came looking for alcohol or drugs."

That didn't add up for me. "In my closet? In my shoes?"

"Where do you suppose they hide their own contraband?" Another shrug. "As I said, 'Kids.' Unless you have got a better explanation."

I spun a slow circle on one heel, imagining the cottage as I'd last seen it, and finished with renewed confidence in my own hypothesis. "A search. That's what it looked like to me. The way I see it, this place had literally been tossed."

With pointed deliberation, Owen Stuart mirrored my movement, spinning a slow circle that ended with another shrug. "Searching for what?" He shook his balding head. "As far as I can see, nothing is missing. What is there to take, anyway?"

My turn to shrug. "When I get that figured out, I expect to know who took it."

Before he could reply, Vanessa emerged from the bathroom, cutting short our exchange. Settling her gear in Sam's room took only a few minutes. Though I braced myself before opening the closet, when I hung up her garment bag, I discovered that Owen had already moved Sam's clothes. Thoughtful guy to spare her that constant, painful reminder. He'd even changed the sheets on the bed and cleaned out the chest of drawers. On our way to join the others in the kitchen, I hung back for a quick look into the closet in the entry and found Sam's clothes, some arrayed on hangers and others neatly folded into boxes below.

The trio gathered around the worn wooden table in Sam's kitchen all rose to their feet when we entered. Owen Stuart made the introductions, leading Vanessa to each in turn. I'd already met Leona Holmes, a wiry silver-haired dynamo who taught junior high classes at the village school, and Grant Williams, a cherub-faced thirty-something physician's assistant who acted as the town's only medicine man. Sam had mentioned Nadine Jackson, a U.S. Army vet hoping to break the gender barrier of radio engineering after racking up some civilian experience at the local affiliate of Alaska Public Radio. Her presence provided one kind of racial diversity to the group, but the gathering itself provided another. In Hydaburg, the Haida villagers provided the Us and the rest of us—black and white, male and female, Texan and Alaskan—provided the Them. Not the kind of Us-and-Them mentality that made for animosity, just a recognition of reality. And so we six had gathered to mourn one of our own.

After the introductions, Leona Holmes splashed contraband jug red into an assortment of glasses. Even in a dry town like Hydaburg, some rituals demand wine. While Grant Williams cut generous helpings of lasagna, Nadine Jackson dished up bowls of tossed salad and Owen Stuart snagged a loaf of garlic bread from the far reaches of the oven. Vanessa teared up again when Leona offered an opening toast, so I kept a close eye on her as the meal progressed. Not that I needed to worry. A few thousand years of history attest to the healing properties of human death rituals. From the days of Neanderthals down to our own, gatherings that celebrate the lost can provide immeasurable relief to the bereaved. When Leona Holmes spotted the tears in Vanessa's eyes, she launched the first reminiscence.

"At first I wasn't sure I wanted Sam Houston Larrabee in my classroom. 'A little too young,' I thought. 'Probably watches MTV on his satellite. Maybe looking for a little squaw to keep house.'" She met Vanessa's harsh stare without flinching. "Oh, but he was the clever one. Came to my classroom with one of his picture books, showing my kids the Haida art in this and that museum. 'Stole your totems,' he said. 'Don't let 'em steal your memory.' That's how he reached the grannies—through the kids. After seeing those pictures, the kids carried his message to their grannies and, for the first time, really heard their tales. Puffed 'em all up, he did. Helped them find pride in their heritage."

For a moment, Leona looked away, blinking back tears, and then she turned her attention to her meal, leaving an opening for Grant Williams. He tossed back his wine and set the glass on the table with a firm clink. "Helped save their lives, too."

He planted his chubby arms on the table and looked straight at Vanessa. "Being from the city, you might not believe we've got the same problems, even in a village this small. But there's so much coming and going in this town, this-a-one heads for Seattle, that-a-one comes on back from up Anchorage way. And what do they bring home with 'em? Drugs. Liquor. AIDS. That's what's got me worried. These people already survived one white man's pestilence. Don't think they can survive another."

Grant Williams propped a hand under his chin. "How do you explain AIDS to a Haida kid? How it hides in the body for years before bursting free, leaving the victim hollowed out and wasting away? 'The *gageets,*' Sam told me. 'The land otter people. All the old-time shamans battled *gageets* for the spirits of the people. You tell 'em AIDS is the modern *gageets* and these people will listen.'" A little smile carved his round cheeks. "Well, at least they're starting to listen. Even had a few fellows stop in for instructions before heading off on the ferry." He dipped his head. "So that's a start, thanks to Sam."

Nadine Jackson rocked back in her chair, pushing away from the table. "I don't have a hero story about Sam; I've got a friendship story."

Anchoring one boot heel on the seat of her chair, she clasped her hands around her leg and rested her cheek on her upraised knee. "Last January, on the fifteenth, he came to the station looking for me at the end of the day and sweet-talked me into that four-wheeler of his. Soon's we shut the doors, he opens a teensy cooler hidden under a blanket and pulls out two cold microbrews that he smuggled in from Anchorage."

Her eyes went a little distant, focusing on something none of us could see. " 'What's the occasion?' I asked, even though I already knew. I'd just heard the National Public Radio feed from Washington, D.C., so I knew all about the fuss people were making Outside. 'This is Dr. King's day,' Sam said, and he lifted his glass toward me. 'He was a good man. Let's not ever forget.' "

She raised her head and smiled. "Not too many women like me claim fellowship with a good old boy from Texas, but I do. Sam Houston Larrabee was my friend. And I'll miss him all the rest of my days."

Across the table, Owen Stuart nodded, his face crumpling into a mask of grief that required no words of explanation. Leona Holmes leaned toward him, wrapping his hand between her own and murmuring words of comfort. Grant Williams moved to the deep porcelain sink and filled it with hot, soapy water, while Nadine Jackson cleared the table.

Vanessa sat silently beside me, her eyes still blurred with tears but free now of the mute bleakness of recent days. Give Owen Stuart credit for that. However buttinsky I found his behavior, he had provided the means to the right end. For the first time since Sam's death, I could look at Vanessa without a helpless sense of panic over the depth of her grief. All of which added yet another reason why the word *murder* seemed permanently stuck in my throat.

7

LONG BEFORE ELECTRONIC MAIL, NEWS TRAVELED at lightning speed through small towns. Which explains why our day began the next morning with a phone call from the village public safety office wanting someone to drop by to pick up Sam's "effects." Vanessa took the call in his bedroom, making all the necessary arrangements before I could intercept the message. I appeared in the doorway carrying a steaming mug of coffee just as she hung up the phone. "What was that all about?"

"Public safety office calling for somebody to come in for Sam's things. I said I'd be down directly." My face must have betrayed alarm because a smile ghosted across her lips as she accepted the coffee. "I know you mean well, sugar, but the time's come for you to let me off the leash. I expect I can make it to town and back without falling to pieces." She raked her red mane out of her eyes with a steady hand. "After all, that's what I'm here for—to settle Sam's affairs."

Since her resignation seemed genuine, I acquiesced to her plan to acquaint herself with the town while rounding up Sam's diving equipment from the public safety office and Coast Guard. After she rattled off in his Land Cruiser, I settled myself at his desk, fired up the Pentium and logged on to the Internet to check my E-mail.

Electronic mail beats snail mail and voice mail by miles. Not only does post office mail take forever, the entire enterprise is too darned cumbersome—"pen" the missive on the word processor, print a hard copy, sign said copy, print an envelope, stamp said envelope and then get the little package into the earliest outgoing mail, which sometimes means driving to a mailbox with the next pickup. As for voice mail, if the kids haven't erased the tape, try sorting through a dozen messages without listening to every blessed word, and if pen and paper aren't handy, prepare to listen to all of those messages *again* while playing transcriptionist, fudging a bit on the spellings but praying the numbers go down in the correct order. Contrast those experiences with the ease of E-mail: messages ordered by date and time of arrival; each line displaying the name of the sender; a one-button reply correctly addressed and signed; and a cyberculture ethic that prizes brevity and simplicity in communication, with a sensible indifference to trivialities like correct spelling and punctuation. Add to all of that the surprising intimacy fostered by on-line communication and only a clueless Cassandra or fearful penmanship teacher could object to that aspect of our brave new world.

After my password cleared, the screen filled with lines of sky blue letters on a royal blue background representing twenty-eight new messages, each numbered, dated and showing the sender's name. I opened my E-mail in order by sender, starting with the messages from my kids. Jake had zapped me nine messages: to say hi; to ask permission to see an R-rated action movie; to express sorrow (and a bit of fear) at news of Vanessa's nephew's death; to tell me he loved me; to let me know I sounded weird when I called from Texas; to crow about an A (his first) on a math test; to boost my spirits with a couple of truly terrible kid jokes; to wonder why he'd seen nothing on the news about the orcas; and to make sure I told Vanessa he was really, really sorry about Sam. Jessie had fired off six messages: to let me know her soccer team, the Arctic Foxes (Gag!), won their first game despite that snot, Valerie; to declare herself shocked and upset by Vanessa's nephew's sudden death; to tell me she loved me; to rant about Valerie's incredibly jerky behavior; to wonder if I still planned to see her game in Juneau on Saturday; and to warn me that Valerie might really mess things up for the team. One message sufficed for Nina, the gist of which she'd told me when she picked me up at the airport in Anchorage. John Doyon also made do with a single message of sympathy for me to forward to Vanessa that extended an offer of any assistance that Tanana Regional Corporation could supply. After reading in order the E-mail from my boss, Boyce Reade, I passed over the half-dozen messages that looked to be strictly routine and composed my replies, saving one message—the only one from overseas—as my reward.

My E-mail to Jake nixed the R-rated movie, offered kudos for his achievement in math, assured him that weirdness is an appropriate reaction to sudden death and reminded him that I loved him to pieces. Jessie received congratulations on her soccer team's first win, reassurance that I would cheer her on in Juneau on Saturday, affirmation of her dismay at Sam's death and a long string of I LOVE YOUs that ended in three dots. After sending simple acknowledgments to Nina and John Doyon, I hammered out a brief proposal for Boyce, suggesting a people hook for the orca story, namely Owen Stuart, the local cetacean biologist whose lifework would be disrupted, if not destroyed, by the taking of twelve whales from the resident pod that provided his research base.

After sending the last reply, I made myself comfortable, relaxing against Sam's chair and opening the E-mail from Konstantin Zorich, a Russian botanist at the New Siberian Experiment Station. *"Krasavista,"* he'd written. "Today on the tundra, in a hollow place warmed by the sun, I found the first flower of spring, with petals pink and soft, and so I thought of you. Like the flower, your skin is soft and pink and fresh in the morning air. And like the tundra flower, you have the courage to struggle for survival, the hope to defeat pessimism and the love to conquer despair. Stand fast and all will be well."

His words loosed a warm tingling flood that renewed and refreshed, leaving me glowing, incandescent, on a chilly spring morning. Konstantin Zorich had come into my life almost a year earlier, and not for the first time since I'd met him, I wished the earth would spin faster on its axis, speeding up time so I could find out, could *know,* if he would be the one who would help me let go of my Max and if I would be the one who would help him let go of his Tatiana. Perhaps that's the ultimate virtue of the on-line world, creating new communities that transcend the boundaries of nations, races, colors and creeds to enable a woman perched on the edge of her continent to become the intimate of a man perched on the edge of his continent a frozen ocean away.

The full-throated growl of the Land Cruiser penetrated the closed windows of Mission Cottage, shattering my reverie. I had planned to thoroughly check the files on Sam's computer, even without any clear idea of what I'd be looking for, but instead I logged off the Internet, shut down the Pentium and went outside to help Vanessa unload Sam's diving gear from the back of his rig.

"Let me give you a hand." I came up beside her, slipping the buoyancy compensator vest over an arm, hoisting the tank to my shoulder and grabbing both fins with one hand.

Vanessa cinched down the mouth of a green plastic

garbage bag, tied off the ends and shoveled the whole ungainly load into her arms. "I think that's everything."

After holding open the door so she could toddle through, I followed her into the living room of Mission Cottage, dropping the flippers onto the scarred surface of an end table and propping the tank against it before settling beside Vanessa on the overstuffed couch with the half-inflated vest spread across my knees. She tossed her hair over her shoulders and went to work on the knot she'd just tied, picking it open with vivid fingernails and then plunging an arm into the garbage bag that gaped on the floor before her. In short order, she dug out Sam's mask and gloves, which she placed on the couch between us before reaching back into the plastic bag.

I picked up the blue rubber mask, turning it over in my hands but, beyond a superb patch job on the nosepiece that attested to Sam's painstaking maintenance of his gear, found nothing out of the ordinary. The gloves told an entirely different story. On the left, a half-dozen nicks scarred the blue neoprene that covered the back of the hand, and five deep cuts grooved the palm of the right. I fingered those slices for a few moments, trying to imagine the source of the damage. The sea scours and softens everything washed by its waters. Granite crags wear into round, tumbling pebbles, and jagged metal blunts enough to crumble at a touch. Only a new wreck, something very recent, would provide the kind of razor-sharp entanglement needed to turn Sam's diving gloves into this tattered mess. Did such a wreck exist? In the middle of Cordova Bay?

"Blast it all!" Vanessa sat back with a huff and gave the garbage bag a swift kick. "If it's in there, I can't find it."

I reached for the bag. "What are you looking for?"

"Sam's knife." Her eyes scrunched, threatening tears. "The one I gave him when he finished college." She swiped a hand across her eyes. " 'Time for you to have some fun, boy.' That's what I told him."

I sat forward, dragged the bag toward me and then dumped it at our feet, tumbling out the shredded remains of Sam's wet suit, which someone had cut from him before his body was sent to Texas. His hood fell out, along with the regulator from his air tank, which sprouted six inches of breathing hose and hit the floor with a clank. I scooped up the regulator and ran a finger across the end of the hose. Nothing snagged my skin. The cut appeared clean, almost surgical, and certainly not the ragged tear I'd expected.

Dropping to the floor on my knees, I lifted the wet suit, sifting through sleeves and legs sliced into tentacles, until I found the shredded remnant of his knife sheath in the tangled remains of the wet suit's right leg. No knife. And what about his weight belt? Another quick search turned up no weight belt. When I'd slid to the floor, the buoyancy compensator vest had come with me, and now I picked it up, examining the half-inflated chambers that had circled Sam's neck like a workhorse's heavy collar, remembering how he'd been found floating facedown on Cordova Bay. The half-inflated vest had lifted him to the surface but contained too little air to roll his face out of the water. Not that that would have saved him. Sam Houston Larrabee died long before his body reached the surface. Or so the Coast Guard theorized.

All the while I'd been scrabbling through Sam's gear, Vanessa had remained silent but watchful, following my every move with keen attention. Now she, too, sat forward. "Lauren, what's wrong? What are you thinking right now?"

Rather than answer, I offered her the regulator from Sam's air tank, along with what remained of the breathing tube that had been his lifeline underwater. After a moment's hesitation, she took the regulator from me and gently circled the severed hose with one finger before stiffening, her face a mask of outrage. "That's not torn. You said his hose was torn."

I stared at the severed hose in her hand, searching with my eyes for what my fingers had already failed to find—any trace of evidence that Sam's lifeline had been torn, not cut. "I thought his hose had torn. I was told that his hose had torn."

Vanessa's eyes flashed with accusation. "Who told you?"

"The commander of the Coast Guard cutter that found him."

Her accusatory eyes provided all the incentive I needed to get to my feet and head for the telephone in Sam's bedroom. She followed me, sinking onto the bed next to me while my call passed up the chain of command until finally reaching Nathan Chaloner. After about thirty seconds, I cut off the chitchat with a very pointed question. "Didn't you say Sam Houston Larrabee's air hose was torn?"

He replied instantly, all business now. "I did indeed."

"Well, Captain Chaloner, I have that air hose right here in front of me, and there's no tear." Beside me, Vanessa nodded vigorously, and I tightened my grip on the receiver. "Looks to me like that hose was severed with one clean cut."

His pause lasted no more than a heartbeat. "Perhaps I misspoke when I talked to you that day in the *Kodiak*'s wardroom. In fact, the hose was cut, and the way I see it, Mr. Larrabee himself did the cutting." I swallowed my surprise and angled the phone so Vanessa could listen in. "You see, his knife is missing. I think he got tangled in something, shredded his gloves while trying to free himself and finally had to use his knife. By that time, he was probably pretty worked up, panicky, and simply forgot to exhale." At the word *panicky,* Vanessa frowned and shook her head. I held up a hand to keep her quiet. "When that air embolism hit his brain, everything let go, including his grasp on the knife. It's still down there somewhere."

All very logical. Even Vanessa's frown vanished. Except . . . "Captain Chaloner, that area where we found him out in Cordova Bay, are you aware of any wrecks out there?"

The tension in his voice evaporated. "Oh, there're

wrecks all through these waters, some dating back hundreds of years. This coast saw lots of action during the age of imperialism. Russia, Spain, France, England—all of them came looking for anything they could get."

"What about more recent wrecks?" Although I managed a neutral tone of voice, Vanessa's frown returned. "Say from the last couple of years?"

"Like I said, there're wrecks all through these waters. We lose ships and boats every year."

"Lose any recently near where Sam was found?"

Now he paused, enough for a three-count. "None I can recall off the top of my head."

"What about his transportation?" Vanessa's frown turned into a glower, and when she opened her mouth to speak, I shushed her with a glare. "Did you find a boat?"

A longer pause this time, enough for a five-count. "No, we did not."

"So how did he get out there without a boat?" I turned my eyes away from the wrath-of-God expression on Vanessa's face. "Do you have any explanation for that?"

Now he sighed deeply, not the kind of sigh that signified impatience with my question but more the kind of sigh that expressed surrender of a sort. "No, I do not. No boat and no explanation." He cleared his throat before continuing. "Mrs. Maxwell, do you have any information about Mr. Larrabee's death that I should be aware of?"

The question reaching my ear didn't skewer me

nearly as painfully as the question in Vanessa's angry eyes. I still hadn't told her about the break-in and search of Sam's house, and somehow that didn't seem the right moment either. Instead, I threw her a chin-up smile before sending a resigned sigh of my own through the telephone wire and into the Coast Guard officer's ear. "I'm afraid not, Captain Chaloner. Looks like I've got lots of questions but no answers to speak of."

Not yet, anyway.

8

Hydaburg's harbor bristled with a growing flotilla that sprouted antennas tuned not only to marine forecasts and fishing market updates but also to the radio newscasts of the networks which continued to ignore the confrontation brewing in the waters off Prince of Wales Island. From around the globe had come an armada of environmentalists vowing to defend the orcas no matter the cost, including the most militant ecowarriors on Earth, many of them spoiling for the mother of all showdowns. The greens on hand included members of Earth First! whose monkey wrenching in the American West inspired federal prosecution in a half-dozen states; Greenpeace, famed for going nose-to-nose with the French over nuclear tests in the South Pacific at a cost of one life, two ships and numerous arrests; Earth Island Institute, which smuggled cameras aboard tuna boats to document dolphin genocide; and the Sea Shepherd Conservation Society, which in 1986 sank half of Iceland's whaling fleet. Activists, in other words, committed to direct action whose presence guaranteed headaches and sleepless nights for all of those who sought a peaceful resolution to the conflict over the orcas, including me. The Wild America Society preferred the weapon of public opinion, but without a compelling news hook for the editors back East, we had no ammunition. The day before, Boyce Reade and I had exchanged a flurry of E-mail about our lack of ammo, including a lengthy consideration of tactical alternatives such as applying pressure to the White House to withhold the capture permits. In the end, his analysis had been unequivocal: "News hook plus public opinion equals pressure stops capture. No news hook equals no public opinion equals no pressure equals twelve orcas captured. *Find that hook!*" Meaning my first order of real business remained locating and sharpening that hook, so at lunchtime I headed into town for a bit a schmoozing at the Sweetland Cafe.

Most small-town Alaska restaurants serve up standard American fare—breakfast and burgers, steaks and spaghetti—with bland church coffee and the usual choices in soft drinks. And like many of the small-town restaurants in the Lower forty-eight, the best food in the place isn't always on the menu. The culinary glory of Sweetland resided in homemade soup and homemade desserts, a fact quickly discovered by the media types whose stay in Hydaburg mostly had consisted of that old army standby—hurry up and wait. When I came through the glass-paned door on a chill gust of wind, those oilcloth-covered tables not already staked out by the press boasted full complements of idle ecoactivists. Behind the counter, the fryers sizzled with wire baskets brimming with french fries, and from the jukebox in the corner, an oldie from Garth Brooks provided a backbeat to the buzz of conversation and clatter of plates and silverware. Beyond the trio who cooked and served the food, nary a Hydaburg native could be seen in the place. Not that the townies minded losing a hangout to the temporary invaders. Alaskan resourcefulness includes taking advantage of the economic benefits of all accidents of nature, whether earthquake, oil spill, tsunami or major news story. Now was the time to cash in on the orcas. There'd be plenty of opportunity to enjoy the pie à la mode at Sweetland when the whale folks went home.

I paused just inside the door to survey the faces that ringed the café's dozen tables, mentally sketching out the most efficient course for trolling with my news hook. I had no time to waste since I was expected aboard the whalehunter's ship in an hour for a long-standing appointment with their head honcho. Following Boyce's advice, I made alternative media my priority and threaded between the tables, stopping here to pitch Owen Stuart to a stringer for CNN—"A man's life's work is at stake!"—and pausing there to cast the idea to a correspondent for a Fox network magazine show—"This guy is America's Jacques

Cousteau!" Start with TV, move to the wire services, then on to the major metropolitan dailies, don't forget the radio networks and finish with the wannabees, freshly minted college graduates who acted as gofers for the real journalists in exchange for the chance—even a very slim one—to do some reporting of their own. Three young guys in flannel shirts and rain gear pushed their chairs away from the wannabee table just when I arrived, leaving me my choice of seats and Kelsey Kavanaugh for company. As I sat down across from her, she tossed me a smile and then nibbled a cracker she'd dipped into her split pea soup.

I snagged a passing waitress and ordered a bowl of soup before addressing my companion. "Any luck placing that film you shot with the Coast Guard last week?"

"Nope." She ripped the cellophane off another pair of crackers and rolled her eyes. "News directors don't want rescues; they want blood."

News directors also wanted glamour pusses with coiffed hair and tailored suits, not waifs with buzzed heads and combat boots, no matter how beautiful their features. Not that I told Kelsey Kavanaugh my amateur assessment. And not that she needed me to tell her the television facts of life. She had, in fact, explained the reality of TV news to me not long after we'd met and simply shrugged when I'd asked why she wanted to make a career in such a dog-eat-dog world: " 'Cause I'm good." Her combination of insight, intelligence and confidence had impressed the hell out of me then; now I described the Owen Stuart news hook I'd pitched to her future colleagues. "How's that sound?"

"Like it could work. On the right day, that is." She leaned toward me, anchoring her elbows on either side of her bowl of soup. "See, the most important element of news is timing. On a slow news day, Hillary Clinton's new haircut is a big fucking deal. On the day Yitzak Rabin gets whacked, who cares?"

I couldn't suppress a sigh. "So you're saying that on top of the fact that everybody's sick of whales and most people can't find Alaska on the map, the orcas are also at the mercy of random violence anywhere on earth?"

"Yup." She nodded briskly but, at the sight of my frown, decided to toss me a crumb. "There's a couple of things you can do to increase your odds of making the air."

I cocked my head. "Like what?"

"Great pictures, for one. Without great film, your story is just another talking head, and there's a strict limit on that in every newscast." She picked up her spoon. "And try to break the story on a Monday. That's the deadest news day of the week, and everybody's scrabbling for anything that's halfway interesting."

After tucking away that advice and finishing my soup, I made my way back outside, pausing at a few tables to pitch Owen Stuart to the news types I'd missed on my way in, hoping that somebody—*anybody*—would figure out a way to make the mild-mannered cetacean biologist into next week's big news story. I'd lived long enough to know that last year's hot news is this year's deadly bore, and I worried a lot that following all the hoopla over *Free Willy,* the current public opinion might run more toward *Can Willy.* But this wasn't just about saving whales; it was about saving people, too. My biggest fear was that this story would deliver the blood coveted by news directors. Although I'd considered myself an ecowarrior since joining the Wild America Society, to the bomb-thrower enviros gathered at Hydaburg, my employer and others of our ilk belonged strictly in the wuss leagues of activism, also known as peacemakers. Which helped explain why I'd decided to spend the afternoon with the villains of the piece, the whale hunters themselves.

A Frenchman biologist named Raoul D'Onofre served as the Ahab of the outfit and his ship, *Le Mistral,* took its name from a famed and reviled Mediterranean wind. In contrast to the aging and often rusty tubs of the environmentalists, the whale-hunter's *Le Mistral* boasted gleaming white paint with blue accents, an impressive array of state-of-the-art electronics and pristine fishing nets just waiting for cetacean prey. A muscular young sailor with a no-nonsense scowl watched over the pier end of the gangplank and declined to let me aboard until someone on *Le Mistral* radioed down permission.

No sooner had I reached the stern deck than the seaman on guard there secured the rail, and the ship began to move, backing slowly away from the Hydaburg docks until the bow had enough leeway to come around onto a heading for the Sukkwan Strait. A tall and lean man with steel gray hair made his way to me across the deck, his wary brown eyes belying the hand he extended toward me. "Mrs. Maxwell! I'm Raoul D'Onofre. Will you be quite comfortable on deck, or would you prefer a seat on the bridge?"

With the Sweetland's finest soup warming my belly, I barely noticed the icy thread in the air. "The deck's fine. What's on the program?"

"Capture drills." He snapped his fingers at a mate who hovered nearby, sending the fellow jogging toward the superstructure that rose amidships, and then indicated the piles of net which took up most of the deck. "To seize the best specimens, we must drill and drill and drill."

Seize. In spite of D'Onofre's sexy accent, the word annoyed me. And although I admired the Frenchman's decision not to mask his purpose behind a veil of euphemism, I couldn't resist the urge to dig a bit beneath his charming surface. "Judging from this boat, seizing marine mammals provides a handsome income. What's the going rate for an orca in its prime?"

The merest flicker of irritation tugged at the corner of his mouth. "In American dollars? Let me think."

The gofer mate returned and handed D'Onofre a slick little radio that he slipped into a pocket of his Gore-Tex parka. "In 1992 a Canadian aquarium paid one hundred forty thousand dollars for a specimen seized in Icelandic waters, but one of your own ocean parks spent one million dollars for another on display in British Columbia."

As *Le Mistral* cleared the harbor, the breeze stiffened. I dug into the front pocket of my anorak for my fleece headband and, after positioning it over my ears, pulled on the matching purple gloves. "How much are you getting for this dozen?"

The Frenchman lifted his chin, thrusting it into the air, while he zipped his parka against the wind. "For the orcas? Three million. With the other specimens—"

"Forget the others." I held up my gloved hand to cut him off and turned back toward the rail to scan the green waters of the strait. "Nobody gives a damn about the other species."

A hundred yards off *Le Mistral,* a black triangle rose from the water, the dorsal fin of an orca, and a small cloud of vapor erupted from the whale. In captivity, those fins collapse, flopping over uselessly, unnecessary for either heat regulation or stability in a temperature-controlled pool without tide or surf. After skimming just below the surface long enough to take three cloud-forming breaths, the whale sounded again, the dorsal fin vanishing beneath the waves.

"Beautiful, eh?" Wonder had replaced wariness in Raoul D'Onofre's brown eyes, which stared off across the water to the place where the orca had swum. "And to think that they are voluntary breathers, who always doze because they must wake to breathe."

I gripped the rail with my hands but couldn't keep

the needling tone from my voice. "So they never really sleep? Bet that makes them hard to seize."

"Yes, it does." He looked back at me, his eyes frankly appraising. "Did you know that we humans are like whales in our diving response? In cold water, the human heartbeat slows and blood flows only to the brain and the heart, much as whales when they dive. As species, whales and humans are alike in many ways."

My hands tightened on the rail. "Knowing that, how can you do this?"

He cocked his head, and a crooked smile curved his lips. "I first met orcas when I was diving in Madagascar. I heard them before I saw them. Their sounds came to me through the water, calling back and forth, and suddenly I realized that someone was there."

I turned to face him then, dropping my hands to my sides. "Someone? Not something?"

"Definitely someone. They visit our world and then vanish into their own, but eventually we will destroy their world." He swept a hand before him, taking in all the waters of the Sukkwan Strait. "Here we come together, in these coastal waters, both species searching for the salmon. For humans, fish can be farmed, but orcas must have wild salmon, and those runs are nearing extinction. Soon the whales of these pods will begin to starve."

I flinched at his grim prediction, not wanting to embrace the worst-case scenario, even though I knew that fishing regulators routinely ignored the needs of orcas. Both Canadian and American fishery managers set their quotas without factoring in the estimated 650 tons of fish each orca consumed in a year. And despite their best efforts to save the salmon, the governments of both countries had recently instituted buy-out programs for fishermen and their boats, in an effort to reduce the salmon fleets to preserve the rapidly dwindling wild runs on the Pacific Coast.

He leaned toward me, his dark eyes glittering with emotion. "And what of the poisons from our human world? What of your *Exxon Valdez?*" He spoke slowly, almost spitting the words out. "Before the oil spilled, an American colleague had singled out one pod of thirty-six orcas for intense study. In the first year after the oil, seven disappeared. In the following year, another six vanished. In two years, one-third of the whales were gone!"

This time I didn't flinch. "Owen Stuart estimates there are sixty resident orcas in southeast Alaska waters, and you plan to take twelve—that's twenty percent gone in one year!"

A little muscle near his eye twitched. "Gone, yes, but not dead. We know enough now to indefinitely preserve this species in captivity. From the research to come, someday perhaps the orcas will return to the wild."

I ground out each word between clenched teeth. "If you don't take them now, maybe they won't have to be returned to the wild someday."

For an endless moment, we stood there by the rail of *Le Mistral,* toe-to-toe in the freshening wind, matching each other glare for glare on the rolling deck, neither of us willing to give in or even back off. I half expected him to taunt me, to ask what kind of a scientist I was, or to throw my gender up in my face, to wonder aloud if all women were so irrational and softheaded? But I didn't need Raoul D'Onofre's questions to enrage me. Behind my outward intransigence, my mind rang with doubts and questions. About the inevitability of confrontation. About the inadequacy of peacemakers. And about this latest spectacular blunder in the long-running drama, *Lauren Maxwell Fails the Whales.*

High above *Le Mistral*'s deck, a blast erupted from a hidden horn. Raoul D'Onofre straightened, the fire in his eyes replaced by an icy determination. "The time for capture drills has come."

9

CAPTURING ORCAS TAKES A BIG NET, A COUPLE OF small runabouts and a strong cage. A June 1965 fishing mishap resulted in the first capture of a killer whale. A gill netter nearing the British Columbia shore cut loose a tangled net, which drifted onto nearby rocks, trapping a pair of orcas in a small cove. An adolescent whale managed to escape and rejoin the rest of the pod, which hovered just behind the cork line that floated the curtain of net, but an enterprising showman herded the mature young male he named Namu into a forty-by-sixty-by-twenty-foot welded cage floated by four dozen oil drums. A barge towed Namu's floating cell to Seattle, trailed by the entire pod, which kept a running chorus of protest, squeaking and bubbling all the way into the dirty harbor where Namu spent the rest of his short life, entertaining tourists and schoolchildren. After that first capture, the hunters tried to improve their technique by harkening back to the Nantucket whalers of old, harpooning orcas with buoyed lines and giving chase, eventually using a fishing boat with nets and easily maneuverable runabouts to corral the tired whales. In the next eight years, whalers captured forty-seven more orcas in British Columbia waters, killing an additional twelve whales in the process.

When Raoul D'Onofre announced the impending drill, I scanned *Le Mistral*'s deck and crew from my spot at the rail, searching for the Greener gun, a harpoon-firing rifle. After coming up empty, I tossed a question to the French Ahab, who'd pulled the radio from his pocket and started firing off orders in his native tongue. "Your harpooner doesn't need to practice?"

His brown eyes narrowed, and his fingers clenched the radio more tightly. "I do not employ a harpooner, Mrs. Maxwell. My purpose is to protect the orcas, not to injure them." A flicker of some new emotion momentarily lit his eyes. "Will you not at least try to keep an open mind? And perhaps consider the validity of an alternative approach to this problem?"

First, he termed the orcas "someone"; now he termed them a "problem." Still, my emotions were getting the better of me. After the turmoil of the last few days, no one could blame me for that. For a moment I looked away, back toward the jagged shoreline of Prince of Wales Island, where the tops of the Sitka spruces swayed with the wind and the worn bow of a fishing boat had just emerged from behind a rocky point. And I did hate fuzzy-wuzzy thinking about wildlife issues—grizzly bears deserve our protection not because they're cute, but because they're magnificent predators crafted by eons of evolution who own a piece of this world, no matter how populous and technological the planet becomes. Yet as a would-be peacemaker, I certainly had no business going around building fences.

I turned back to the whale hunter and stuck out my hand. "You're right, Dr. D'Onofre. I should keep an open mind, and I will. From here on out, I'll forgo the wisecracks and just watch."

Just watching proved excruciating, however. I followed Raoul D'Onofre to the stern of the ship, taking up position next to him on an elevated platform well clear of the piled net. First, *Le Mistral* lowered a motorized Zodiac raft into the water, which took the part of the targeted orca. When the Zodiac moved toward a shallow cove, the whaling ship cruised into position beside one of the cove's headlands before launching a small runabout that headed toward the beach dragging the end of a six-hundred-fathom net. The net stretched out into a bulging U, encircling the Zodiac. Soon the Zodiac reacted, zooming toward the end of the net, trying to escape before the circle closed. But when the Zodiac made its run, another runabout cut it off, forcing the motorized raft back into the belly of the narrowing U. In order to keep running, the Zodiac risked a collision in a seaborne game of chicken, and so the helmsmen turned off, allowing the net to complete the capture. To my inexperienced eyes, *Le Mistral*'s crew had performed a flawless capture drill. To Raoul D'Onofre, their practice left much to be desired, particularly the performance of the Zodiac's helmsman. The Frenchman yanked the radio out of his pocket and barked out rapid-fire orders. An observer didn't need to be fluent in French to understand that message. Pissed off sounds the same in any language.

Within minutes, the Zodiac's young skipper appeared on deck, a rugged-faced sailor whose blond hair dripped sea spray. As he approached D'Onofre, he unbuckled his life vest and loosened the sealed neck of his heavy orange survival suit. *"Mon capitaine?"*

As the winch racketed to life, winding in the long, dripping net, the Frenchman's tirade added a bellowing counterpoint, a machine-gun sputtering of outrage and fury that would have withered most men. While other crewmen kept their distance, the young sailor simply listened, his paling face the only hint of his upset. Although I couldn't understand the words of Raoul D'Onofre's harangue, I read loud and clear the message in the Zodiac skipper's reaction, or lack thereof. I'd seen similar disassociation in children many times, especially kids trapped in homes headed by angry men or women. The eyes never waver, but the focal point moves far away to a safe place where parents don't scream, and the body remains still, but the practiced eye detects a vibrant alertness prepared to fight or flee. My take on Raoul D'Onofre instantly changed from misguided biologist to insufferable autocrat. I have learned through bitter experience that screeching gets you nowhere, and despite—or because of?—my own sorry history of temper tantrums, my response to all abusive bullies never wavers. I just walk away.

Aboard *Le Mistral* I couldn't get too far, moving only to the end of the elevated platform, and then I also disassociated, focusing across the open water to the worn old fishing boat that had anchored just outside the cove used in the drill. A black-haired man, stocky in his bright yellow rain suit, appeared on deck, his dark face turned toward the whaling ship. Probably a Haida fisherman, maybe wondering if the orcas to be captured could possibly be relatives. The Haidas believed that men who drown come back to life as killer whales and that the orcas ruled the Ocean people who lived under the sea. Long ago, the Haida feared the Ocean people and their chief, Killer Whale, a fisherman who one day went to sea in his canoe and never returned. The killer whales lived in towns near steep cliffs and rocky headlands and grabbed passing Haidas, dragging them under the sea as they had taken the fisherman who became their chief. But the chief always remembered the Haida and wanted to relieve them of their fear of orcas. So he held a great feast, inviting all the world's chiefs, the monsters of the sea and the earth and the upper world, who arrived using killer whales as their canoes. When the chief told the ocean monsters of the sorrow they caused the Haida, the orcas moved their homes away from the waters traveled by fishermen and stopped dragging the Haida from their canoes. Ever after, the descendants of that great chief carved their totem poles with orcas to commemorate his brave deed.

As I stared across the dark water, studying the descendant of that great chief who stood motionless at the railing of his small fishing boat, I realized gradually that D'Onofre had stopped shouting, leaving not silence but the groan of the laboring winch, the slap of the wet net against the deck and the scream of a gull that wheeled above *Le Mistral.* After a few more minutes, the winch sputtered and sighed and fell silent. Then the Zodiac raced back into the cove, and the drill began again.

This time the Frenchman watched his crew through binoculars that hid every part of his face except his mouth, lips firmly pressed into a stern line of displeasure. As the first runabout began its work, tugging the soggy net from the deck of the ship, I took a deep breath and let it out slowly, trying to release the tension that gripped and stiffened me.

Out on the water, the swollen waves from the wake of the net dragger rolled toward the Zodiac, and the second runabout entered the chase, angling toward the streaking raft that tried to outrace the closing net. As the boat and raft converged, still trailing the runabout dragging the net, the swollen wake of the net dragger reached them, hitting broadside. The herding runabout steadied on, but the Zodiac raft teetered atop the swell and then tipped into the trough, hanging perpendicular to the water, sliding sideways toward the runabout, surfing down the swell on one tube.

High side!

As if responding to my silent scream, the raft's helmsman threw himself across the Zodiac to provide a counterbalance, clawing for purchase as the high side rose up, up, up and over. As the raft flipped, the Zodiac launched the driver, throwing him clear, a streak of orange that rocketed into the frigid water, vanishing beneath the waves.

"Shit!" Had he tightened the collar of his survival suit? Had he buckled his life vest? Even if he had, he couldn't last long in water that cold. I grabbed Raoul D'Onofre's sleeve. "Get him out of the water pronto!"

The Frenchman dropped the binoculars but made no reply, instead barking orders into the radio in his hand. The ship's horn bellowed—six separate blasts—and crewmen scrambled across the deck.

I rose up on my toes, scanning the chop of green water; searching for orange this time, a piece of the sun, and swept by a sickening sense of déjà vu. Not another floater!

The net dragger slowed to a stop, riding the swells, while the other runabout spun a tight circle, dodged past the flipped Zodiac with its propeller now raised to the sky, and made for the spot where the helmsman disappeared.

"Do you see him?" Raoul D'Onofre repeated the question into his radio. "Does anyone see him?"

"Le voilà!" On the deck below, a sailor froze in

place with his arm outstretched, on point like a hunting dog. *"Le voilà, mon capitaine!"*

Buoyed by his vest and survival suit, the raft's helmsman bobbed in the water, a floating orange beacon, as the runabout came up at his side. The dry driver quickly fished his comrade out of the Sukkwan Strait, and then the pair circled back to the flipped Zodiac raft. On the deck of *Le Mistral,* the winch growled to life, spooling in the net, and the incident was over.

Not that my heart figured that out right away. A shot of adrenaline had ratcheted up my pulse, and although I'm in pretty good shape, slowing my heartbeat took awhile. Even though I'd gotten over my fear, anger still billowed through me. The entire episode had been stupid, pointless and totally avoidable, which is exactly what I told Raoul D'Onofre, my voice ringing with fury. "Risking real lives in a drill is absolutely irresponsible! What kind of man are you?"

"A very deliberate one, Mrs. Maxwell." His voice matched mine in wrath. "That sailor was never in danger. And when we have an orca in our sights, there must be no mistakes."

He climbed down the ladder, each step clanging against the metal, and left me alone on the elevated platform. Looked like our temporary truce had just collapsed, racking up yet another triumphant failure to report to my boss. Not that I particularly cared at that moment. That would have required more calm than I could claim.

I turned my face away from the wind, again settling

my gaze on the Haida fishing boat anchored near the cove, but my mind raced on, unheeded by the picturesque view. What kind of man was Raoul D'Onofre? The kind who'd put a man at risk unnecessarily. Could that willingness to risk lives to capture the orcas extend to murder? But what threat would a historian like Sam Houston Larrabee pose to the French biologist or to anybody else? With that question, I reached the heart of the mystery—find the motive to find the murderer.

The sudden insight momentarily settled my mind, leaving my vision clear and focused on the fishing boat riding at anchor, and the Haida fisherman still watching *Le Mistral* from the bow. Suddenly a tongue of fire flickered behind the windshield of the pilothouse. The Haida fisherman flinched and began to turn. But before he could, the man and his boat dissolved in one thunderous and blinding flash.

10

The orange blossom of flame billowed into a burning cloud, flashing with millions of glittering sparks and wreathed with wisps of black smoke. An invisible wall of wind slammed into me, tossing me back against the waist-high railing of the elevated platform. The metal bar caught me just above the hip, doubling me over. The air teemed with a fog of wind-whipped grit that stung eyes and cheeks and hands, and the raw tang of petroleum fuel soured the air. For a moment, the sky rained debris—a twisted length of aluminum, a jagged stick of wood, a cracked shard of plastic—and then an eerie quiet fell. Within seconds, a cacophony of shouts shattered the sudden silence.

I lifted myself off the railing, moving slowly because of the pain in my side. Raoul D'Onofre raced up the ladder from the deck. "Mrs. Maxwell? You are hurt?"

"Not really. Just a little banged up." My ears ached

from the terrible thunder clap, and when I finger-combed my hair, my hands raked up slivers of debris. "How about your crew?"

"The men are fine, thanks be to God." He swung an arm toward the cove where the Haida fishing boat had been anchored and shrugged. "But the fisherman . . ."

I nodded and held out one hand, displaying the slivers combed from my hair. "Blown to bits."

For the first time since the force of the blast had hit me, I looked out over the water. Debris pocked the surface of the sea, strewn thickly like a ring around a bull's-eye, but in the center—where the boat had been—the swells had been swept clean. *Le Mistral*'s runabouts had survived the blast, and all three helmsmen appeared unhurt, but each boat boasted a windshield spider-webbed with shattered glass. The overturned Zodiac listed in the water, one tube pierced and deflating fast, and the propeller column of her outboard motor displayed a new, corkscrew twist. I turned back to the Frenchman. "What do you suppose happened?"

"A buildup of fumes in the bilge and then a spark?" He gave another very Gallic shrug. "Who can tell? Your Coast Guard, perhaps. Until they arrive, we will remain on station and search for survivors."

A mere formality but the search steadied all hands, including mine. I followed Raoul D'Onofre down to the deck, and when he ducked into the pilothouse, continued on to the bow of *Le Mistral*. The echo of the explosion rang in my ears, and a vision of the

Haida fisherman's face kept appearing in my mind's eye, leaving my hands and knees trembling.

I found a sheltered spot beside a funnel and slid to a seat on the deck, my back braced against the sturdy metal. When a blast crumpled the foundation of the World Trade Center, many Americans learned for the first time what people in Belfast and Paris and Jerusalem had known for decades—a big enough explosion can knock the world on its ear. And after a crude fertilizer bomb sheared the front off the federal building in Oklahoma City, we learned that it didn't take a nuclear bomb to obliterate a human being. But learning isn't necessarily knowing. In the flesh, *vaporize* is an ugly, brutal word. I crossed my ankles and clasped my hands, trying to still the involuntary shivers, but my gut continued to jiggle like Jell-O.

Out of the wind in the lee of the funnel, the sun's heat finally reached me, so I closed my eyes and lifted my face toward its warmth, willing myself to think of something—*anything*—besides the death I'd just witnessed. When the world seems bleakest, my kids provide a lifeline. So I deliberately thought of them. Jessie, my smart and saucy daughter, who I'd be seeing the next day. And, God, did I need to see my kid. I needed to fold her into my arms, feel that oh-so-soft cheek under mine, and siphon off a bit of her vibrancy to revive my own. From the day of her birth, when twin rainbows appeared in the sky outside my hospital room, Jessie had been a sweet girl, and I sometimes thought of her as my reward for giving birth to Jake. My megawatt son could wear out any dozen parents with his intensity. Not that he's a problem child—Jake has never gotten into trouble—but he's so ardent and headstrong about his enthusiasms, I'm forever oh-so-slightly anxious on his behalf. Even as an infant, Jessie had been my refuge, and her gentle hugs and sweet kisses kept me grounded. I'd always known that if I bungled the job of raising my kids, nothing else I did in my life would much matter, but I'd never really worried about screwing up with Jessie. Jake can be passionate and indomitable, a truly scary combination for even a grizzly bear mother like me. Jessie is rational and just, a dream combination that makes raising her easy and fun. Until now. Tomorrow I'd fly up to Juneau to watch her play soccer and scope out the problem Nina had perceived. And I'd store up plenty of hugs to strengthen me for the battles that surely lay ahead.

An hour later, *Le Mistral* tied up at the wharf in Hydaburg, and Raoul D'Onofre walked me to the gangway and offered me his hand. "Shall we agree to disagree, Mrs. Maxwell?"

"Looks like we've got no choice." I gave his hand one firm shake. "Will the damage to your small boats throw you off schedule?"

Another fluid shrug of his wide shoulders. "Perhaps a few days, but we still are without permits. If your government acts quickly, we will be ready. New boats are just a ferry away." He swept a hand wide to embrace the entire harbor. "And here are many boats, with some for hire."

Among those many boats was another, older Zodiac

raft, this one captained by Owen Stuart, the cetacean biologist I hoped would provide the news hook to lure public attention to the orcas' plight. But when he stomped toward me down the pier, his red face torqued with a scowl that left him looking more like Dr. Demento than the absent-minded professor, a wave of relief swept over me that the national press corps was not, at that moment, on hand. "Traitor!" He spat the word from ten paces, glaring first at me, then at *Le Mistral* and then back at me. "Sell out!"

"Whoa, Dr. Stuart." I held up both hands palm first, mirroring the ancient gesture that shows no intent to harm. His preemptive strike reminded me of the one I'd launched a few hours earlier against Raoul D'Onofre, and the memory left me very uncomfortable. That discomfort, combined with my aching hip and ringing ears, doused the spark of anger that flickered inside me. I was just too tired to take offense, especially when the offending party was also my news hook. And peacemaking *was* my first priority. "Sounds like you've got the wrong idea about my visit with Raoul D'Onofre."

He stopped about three feet from me, fists clenched and bristling with anger. I lowered my hands to waist level and took a step toward him. "Let's talk this out. Why don't we grab a coffee at Sweetland?"

Without a word, he spun on his heel and stalked back the way he'd come, heading straight for his battered old motorized raft. I followed, of course, and offered a string of conciliatory words, trailing behind him like a little lapdog at full yap. A glance at *Le*

Mistral confirmed my fear that the French whale hunter had lingered at the rail to take in the spectacle, and that knowledge gave my words a desperate edge that finally got through to Owen Stuart. "When the good guys start fighting among themselves, the bad guys always win. We've both seen that happen too many times. Don't let it happen here, Owen. Let's talk this out!"

He stopped beside his Zodiac and tossed a glance over his shoulder, taking in a quick view of D'Onofre looking down at us from the rail of his ship. "I do not have time for this. I have work to do."

"Maybe I can help." I circled around Owen Stuart until we stood face-to-face on the wooden pier. "What can I do?"

After an endless moment, he heaved a deep sigh and inclined his head toward the front of the raft, where a snarl of line lay on the deck. "I had to pull a broken hydrophone. Now it is fixed, but I can not put it back in place with that line."

Without asking Stuart's permission, I stepped over the gunwale and into his raft. "I'll straighten it out." My voice fairly chirped—from yapping dog to tweeting bird in under ten seconds! "Can't be tangled any worse than half of my gold chains."

In answer, he just shrugged. Then he climbed into the center of the Zodiac, where the inboard motor lay exposed amid a scatter of tools. The cetacean biologist picked up a wrench and bent over the motor, and I settled myself on the bench seat in the bow, shifting around to find a comfortable seat on the cracked upholstery and then filling my lap with a tangle of marine rope.

My third fingernail was history by the time Owen Stuart started talking. For the first few minutes, he'd clanged his tools against each other like a sullen toddler, but I'd ignored him and the harbor hubbub, working vigilantly to unravel the torturous rope puzzle. He began with a mumble so low that I figured him to be cursing the motor which just sputtered and coughed when he tried the starter. Then the mumble became a mutter with a few distinct words—*orcas, sacrifice, expertise*—and I listened more closely. "I had tenure! A lifelong sinecure! But I gave it up for the chance to do the definitive fieldwork, to become *the* expert on orcas. And I am."

Owen Stuart paused to sort through the tools spread on the deck where he knelt, and I loosened a figure-eight knot, slowly drawing in line to unloop the tangle. The biologist lifted a screwdriver, considered it for a moment, then leaned back to the motor and started muttering again. "Blood money. That is what it is. Damn that Frenchman, damn his underwriters, damn them all! I will not sell out my pods."

I stopped working the rope. "What have they offered you?"

At the sound of my voice, Owen Stuart froze, and I realized that he'd forgotten that I was on board. He swiped a hand across his forehead before turning to me, and the gesture left a smear of grease. "Permanent funding. D'Onofre proposed a long-term contract to underwrite my research. Ten years!" He pointed the screwdriver at the side of the raft. "And equipment! A new raft, state-of-the-art technology, computer time for exhaustive analysis."

The wake of a boat that had just passed finally reached us, gently rocking the Zodiac and lifting one side into the pier—*clunk, clunk, clunk.* Owen Stuart threw out both arms to steady himself. "What did he offer you?"

"Not a damned thing." I gave him a grin. "Imagine that!" My smile slipped a bit. "What did Sam have to say about D'Onofre's offer?"

Owen Stuart snorted. "Sam? Sam didn't care about whales. Sam cared about people. And diving. And look what it got him."

A little pang tweaked my heart. First Sam, now the Haida fisherman—a lot of death for a tiny Alaskan town. I pushed the thought away. "Must have been hard to turn down such a generous offer. Sam told me you didn't have an academic appointment, that you were independent by choice."

The biologist lowered himself to the deck, leaning against the gunwale and resting his grubby hands in his lap. "Occasional fieldwork was not enough with orcas. To take the research to the next level, I had to live in the field, so I gave up my university appointment and moved here. That was twenty years ago."

He turned his face toward the shore, scanning the town sprawled across the waterfront as if measuring the change wrought by the passing of a generation. "I left everything behind for the orcas, but when I first arrived, I would have accepted D'Onofre's offer. I probably even would have helped him cull the pods."

He glanced at me and then lowered his eyes to the dirty hands in his lap. "Now the whales are all that I have. They're both friends and family. After living among the orcas for twenty years, I can not turn my back on them now."

CUT!

My mind trumpeted the word but not a sound escaped me. Not that I have the bona fides in film directing or production. But, like most of my countrymen, the all-pervasive television has taught me a bit about production values. After all, TV is now more American than Mom or apple pie. And many of us seem to move through the days as if we're starring in the movie of our own lives. All of which means I knew a great sound bite when I heard one. And Owen Stuart's monologue struck me as a winner. When I got back from Juneau, I'd dig up a camera in time for take two.

11

Flying into Juneau always exhausts me. That's because landing a jet on the narrow strip of flat ground at the base of Mount Roberts requires aerial maneuvers that demand full concentration and leave no room for error. From my seat in the passenger cabin, I wind up doing my best to help the other pilot: watching our zooming shadow through my window to gauge ground speed, checking the position of the flaps on the wing to judge the correct angle, craning my neck to see out the other window to make sure the plane's on the correct approach. Coming into Juneau, I only sit still at night or when fog blankets the runway.

On the Saturday morning of Jessie's soccer match, a merciful fog that hugged all of southeast Alaska left me free during the one-hour flight to contemplate how and why so many American parents, including me, go gaga over kids' sports. Not so long ago, ambitious parents bragged that little Johnny read his first book on his third birthday or that darling Suzy could do long division with seven-digit numbers by the age of five. In those days, academic excellence—aka brains—inspired parents' rapture. These days, in the *Just Do It* world according to Nike, even the most academically accomplished parents trade boasts about athletic feats—aka brawn. Good old Dad persuades the local cop to bring the radar gun out to the baseball field to clock the Little Leaguers' pitches, and dear sweet Mom lobbies the local editor to send a reporter out to the football field to write up Pop Warner results. Long ago, competitive sports reigned only in high school where speculation centered on which players would make the varsity squad. Nowadays, competition heats up in elementary school where speculation centers on which players will receive full-ride college scholarships. In soccer, the magic word is *select,* designating those kids' teams that hold tryouts and play a more difficult schedule, including plenty of out-of-town tournaments. Which explains how my soon-to-be nine-year-old daughter found herself racking up frequent flyer miles on Alaska Air and sending my VISA bill into the low four figures. "Why" is an entirely different question.

After takeoff, I leaned my forehead against the airliner's window, catching the little buzzing thrum of vibration through the thick plastic, and gazed down at the dense layer of cotton-gauze clouds which co-

cooned the mountains and sea below. For lucky kids, childhood used to be a cocoon of sorts, a safe haven from the sharp edges of the adult world. These days parents go life-and-death on kids' sports for one simple reason—money. No professional sport remotely resembles rocket science in difficulty or in importance, but in a rational universe, the salaries earned by famous jocks could cause some confusion. The 1990s will see multiyear contracts in baseball and basketball surpass thirty million, and a first-time visitor to Earth might be excused for thinking the stakes involved must be akin to the life-or-death games of the Mayans. When my son, Jake, first played soccer, his coach polled the kids and discovered every one of them expected to be a professional athlete someday. Turned out that about a third of the moms and dads had the same expectation. After hearing that, the coach did a bit of research and informed his teams' parents that statistics suggested their sons had twice as much chance of growing up to be neurosurgeons than they had of growing up to be professional athletes. "So let's all just relax, and have fun," he suggested. The next season the team had a new coach.

The flight attendant arrived with the drinks cart, and I reached across the empty seats beside me for a bottle of orange juice and a plastic cup filled with ice. Not that Max or I ever held any illusions about our kids' future as athletes. Before his death, Max made all the decisions about their sports because he had all the experience. In my childhood, girls didn't compete, or at least not in athletics. In high school, girls became cheerleaders or played in the marching band, limited to the role of faithful acolyte while the boys had all the fun and got all the glory. I played plenty of sandlot baseball when I was a kid, but my athletic career abruptly ended when the neighborhood boys reached the minimum age for Little League. Talk about being pissed off! Even today, I effortlessly summoned back the rage and shame and humiliation that roared through me when my mother tried to explain why girls couldn't join Little League. Which probably spells out why my daughter found herself jetting around Alaska to play soccer.

The cold orange juice didn't quite kill my high-altitude cotton mouth, so I sucked on a hollow ice cube and let it melt over my tongue. A few years earlier, a soccer coach had wanted Jake to try out for his select team, but after discussing it, Max and I decided against it. "Let him have fun. Sports should be fun for kids. And maybe it stays that way for girls. But for boys, sports do turn into a manhood thing—the first of many," he told me. "He's just a kid, for God's sake! Let him have fun. He'll get to all that guy stuff soon enough." Jessie's father hadn't lived long enough to make a similar call for her. Not that Max would have automatically ruled out select soccer. "They aren't equal, Lauren. Jake and Jessie aren't the same kid," he'd said when I worried about developing a universal approach to childrearing. "Looks like we'll have to operate on a case-by-case, kid-by-kid basis, or else go nuts trying to balance the scales." A kid-by-kid approach made sense at the time, and still did, but also left me guessing what Max would have done about Jessie's invitation to play select soccer.

The question dogged me the rest of the way to the Juneau field where Jessie's Arctic Foxes faced off against a team of older girls. Older and bigger! A warm spring sun had melted the fog and dried the grass, and when I arrived at the field behind an old wooden school, both teams had started their warm-ups. I circled the field, bright with fresh May grass, and crossed behind the opposing team's parents, heading for the small rooting section the Foxes had brought down from Anchorage. A casual comparison of the girls showed that only Jess equaled the other team's players in height. Before I could make a more detailed analysis of size, another contrast between the two teams distracted me.

"Would you get a look at those outfits!" A skinny woman in a sheepskin-lined Levi's jacket jerked a thumb in the direction of my daughter's team. "Matching warm-ups, no less. And look at those sports bags! They must have dropped two hundred bucks on each kid."

The thin woman's friend shushed her as I walked past with burning cheeks. More like $250 if you added the cost of the cleats. At the corner of the field I paused to study the Arctic Foxes' bench, where a rank of crisp, new navy sports bags marked the perimeter and two parents erected a five-by-eight navy and white banner depicting a cute little female fox in cleats blasting a soccer ball beneath the words Arctic Foxes, Anchorage.

Out on the field, the Juneau girls ran through their drills, dribbling and passing and shooting, each wearing a cotton T-shirt and the recreation league's standard black shorts. Some wore white cleats, others black, and their knee socks boasted a rainbow's array of color. As they drilled, laughter provided frequent punctuation and their voices trilled with high spirits. Even from a distance, the Foxes offered a sadder, sorrier spectacle. Jess and her teammates had stripped off their expensive warm-up suits and now wore the matching jersey, shorts and socks featured by this year's "in" European manufacturer, all color-coordinated navy and white to match their sports bags and team banner, and the whole team looked darling. But just as Nina had warned me, those little darlings acted more like whining snots, with only the occasional taunt to break up the monotony of their world-weary resignation. The Juneau girls cavorted on the field with true enjoyment, seeming to glory in the warmth of the golden sunlight, their steps light and faces bright. On the other side of the field, not even Jessie showed a spring in her step. Not until she spotted me.

"Mom!"

The thrill in her voice sent a thrill through me. She ignored the ball rolling her way and took off running, galloping across the field with arms flung wide.

A couple of her teammates turned to watch, and

one, the coach's daughter, Valerie, shouted in protest, "Jessie, you get back here now. You better listen. I'm captain this week!"

My daughter's steps never slowed until she barreled into me, almost knocking me down. She threw her arms around me, and I tightened mine around her, and then we teetered for a second. When I regained my balance, I gave her a little squeeze. "How you doing, baby?"

For a second, she snuggled her head against my chest, and then she reared back in my arms, a frown marring her rosy cheeks. "Valerie's such a pain!" She pressed her face against me. "But now you're here, Mama. So everything's great!"

The referee tweeted his whistle, calling the teams to the center of the field for a cleat inspection, and Jess scampered off. She ignored the glare that Valerie sent her way and, without a word to her teammates, took up position at the end of the line. When had Jessie and Valerie stopped being friends? They'd known each other since preschool. When Valerie's dad formed the select team, he called Jessie right off, offering her a spot on his roster without even trying out and explaining that a select team of eight-year-olds wouldn't work without my daughter's strategic sense. He'd built his team around Jessie and Valerie, and now nothing passed between them except hatred.

I continued my circuit of the field, dodging the puddles left by the morning's rain, and as I did, I toted up all the dollars spent for Jessie's uniforms, pictures, registration fees, soccer camps and travel.

When I joined the three other mothers at the Foxes encampment, I greeted them with my tally. "Do you know how much we've spent on this game in the last year? Just under two thousand dollars. We must be out of our minds."

A pretty, thirty-something blonde shrugged off the observation. "This is Tonya's dream. This is her future. I'll spend whatever it costs."

Her little girl did have talent—for Alaska. And Alaska has produced some world-class athletes. But soccer doesn't provide much of a future, even for America's best male athletes, let alone the women. Still, Tonya's mom, who juggled kids from two marriages, a new husband, a waitressing job and studies at Anchorage Community College, dreamed of a way out for her daughter, a different future.

Beside her, Liz's mother flashed a meek, ingratiating smile. "I'm not so worried about the future or the money. Liz wants to play so much, and I don't know what she'd do if I said no." She glanced from face to face, gauging our reactions. "At least they're having fun. And they're winning!"

Out on the field, our soccer players circled their coach as he read off the starting lineup and assigned positions. The starters all grinned and a few traded high fives, but those not chosen to start the game walked toward the sideline, shoulders slumping. I inclined my head in their direction. "Not having much fun now."

Virginia's mom, a slim, willowy woman with a

lined face and calm blue eyes, nodded slowly. "But that's part of what they should be learning. Nothing is all fun; everything has a hard part. Learning to cope with the hard parts of life in order to reach the fun reward is the whole point, isn't it?"

Her question remained unanswered when a sharp blast of the referee's whistle signaled the start of the game. Jessie held her ground in the middle of the field, a permanent starter as sweeper with the job of directing the defense and feeding the ball to the offense. In the goal behind the other defenders, Valerie stalked back and forth, toes scuffing and lips pouting. She liked to score, not guard the goal, and Jessie claimed that Valerie sometimes missed the ball on purpose so her dad would put her out on the field.

As the Juneau team began their advance down the field, passing the ball to the wing and threading through defenders toward the Foxes' goal, the coach's daughter appeared unconcerned. First one then another of her teammates failed to stop their advance. And then my Jessie streaked across the grass, her face a mask of grim determination, and deftly intercepted the ball, taking it wide around one Juneau player and another before booting it to the opposite side of the field with a hard pass that dropped right in front of Tonya. Perfect!

My heart soared. "Way to go, Jess!"

There's nothing quite so wonderful as watching your kid do something so totally right. Not that Jess seemed to care. Instead of following up her pass, she spun around and dashed back toward the goal, engaging Valerie in a short but furious exchange that left them both red in the face.

I glanced at the coach, who hadn't noticed. He stood rigid on the sideline, poised beside the white strip of chalk in the grass with a clipboard clenched in his hand, shouting at Tonya to pass to Liz, his voice a mixture of dread and desperation. The women beside me watched with equal solemnity, faces not animated with enjoyment but stiff with anxiety, a line of wraiths worthy of a Greek tragedy. On the field, the girls craned forward as if the intensity of their desire could propel the ball into the net. And when Tonya fired her shot, not at Liz, who stood open on the other side of the goal, but at the knot of defenders arrayed in front of her, a collective groan rose from her teammates, her coach and her fans when the ball ricocheted harmlessly off the shin guards of a Juneau player.

And so the game went. Each time the Foxes brought the ball to the net, a selfish forward in search of glory took a bad shot rather than pass to an open teammate. And each time the Juneau girls brought the ball to our net, passing to whoever had an open shot, Valerie moved a bit more slowly. After letting in three goals, her dad put her back on the field, but even the most brilliant offense couldn't rescue the Arctic Foxes. Not that my daughter's team showed much brilliance. Time and again, girls took the selfish shot rather than pass the ball to a teammate. Instead they shared only sharply hissed comments and narrow-eyed glares. Just before the final whistle, Valerie charged across the field after the ball and, with a skillfully thrown hip, sent Jessie headlong into the ground.

After the obligatory handshakes with the opposing team, Jessie stomped up to me in full huff, a trickle of blood snaking down from a fresh cut on her knee. "I hate Valerie." Her once-sparkling eyes now flamed with nothing but anger. "And if she says one word to me, I'll punch her in the face."

I looked beyond Jessie's angry eyes to her coach, who nursed his own disappointment, and to her teammate's moms, whose definition of future and fun and penance seemed so alien to me, and I realized that without me, my daughter was on her own this weekend, defenseless against the battle that would follow today's disaster. I could imagine the scene in the motel, the grown-ups rationalizing that "girls will be girls" while the players traded venomous glares and barbed taunts as they selected the scapegoat who would bear the blame for the day's loss. Tonight some of the girls would cry themselves to sleep, and then tomorrow afternoon, after a rematch with the jolly Juneau girls, the sullen Arctic Foxes would fly home to Anchorage where the parents assembled at the airport would first ask, "Did you win?" and only later inquire, "Did you have fun?" Fun? As if. No way I wanted my daughter to be among that dreary crew.

Dropping down onto one knee, I held her out at arm's length, studying her angry eyes. "Instead of punching Valerie out, why don't you come back to Hydaburg with me? I know a couple of orcas who'd like to meet a mermaid like you."

"Do you mean it?" All trace of anger evaporated, and her eyes now glistened with a genuine enthusiasm that had been absent far too long. Nina was right. What my kid needed was some real fun.

At my nod, she threw herself against me. "Oh, Mama, you're the best."

I drew Jessie against me and nuzzled my face against her damp, hot cheek. Maybe not the best but trying.

12

NOTHING LIKE HAVING THE FBI TURN UP TO PUT the kibosh on my daydream of blissful bonding between mother and daughter. Before the fed showed up, our return to Hydaburg had actually proceeded with the seamless perfection of a daydream—available seats, easy connections and on-time arrivals. Through it all, Jessie vented her anger, shame, humiliation and remorse over the twin losses of her friendship with Valerie and her love for soccer. The bliss of childhood turns into the nightmare of adolescence far too early these days. Jessie's complaint centered on the classic phenomenon of in-groups and out-groups. Girls can be cruel enforcers, and when Jess refused to shun others, she transformed herself into the Arctic Foxes' primary outcast. Which had the effect of redoubling my daughter's determination to stick it out. "I won't quit the team until I'm good and ready."

The glint in her eyes reminded me of cold, hard ice. "Valerie can get as mean as she wants, but I won't let her win. I'm way more tough than she is."

When we climbed out of the seaplane at Hydaburg in the early evening, the sun still hung in the sky, and I decided to walk Jessie home, giving her a chance to learn the layout of the village while providing a distraction from her one-girl grievance committee. Successful venting requires a monologue, and although I'm all for letting my kids talk things out without offering advice or solutions, the parental art comes in knowing when and how to change the subject. A dozen years of experience had taught me that a change of scenery often works, especially when the new locale features a forest of carved totems.

I shouldered her bag and, at the end of the pier, pointed in the direction of Mission Cottage, turning her away from the commercial part of town, but I let Jessie set the pace. First she paused to admire a Haida dugout that rode at anchor, a craft I hadn't seen before, which featured a carved and painted eagle on the bow. Then she started off briskly, sauntering along the shore road and eager to see Vanessa, but her steps slowed as she struggled to identify the brightly painted creatures adorning one house. "There's a killer whale—see his grin?" She pointed, sweeping the aim of her finger down the length of the house, and ignored both the incongruous satellite dish and the wail of an infant that poured out the open window. "And that's a beaver! Look at his teeth! And his tail."

Around the next corner, she spotted a silvered mortuary pole and darted ahead, dodging around a battered pickup truck and exchanging only a token nod with an old woman who sat on the stoop of her small, cedar plank house, basking in the golden light of early evening. "Look, Mom! Raven's got the clam."

As I passed, the Haida elder raised one hand. I matched her gesture, and then we both smiled. A few yards down the street, I stopped beside my daughter, gazing up at the weather-mellowed red cedar and the mythic bird which appeared to be clasping a rock in one claw. "Why do you think it's a clam?"

"Because that's the Haida story." She went up on tiptoes, her finger tracing the air to make me see the pole her way. "See the groove? That's where the clam shell is open and inside are all the people."

I resettled her sports duffel on my other shoulder. "Maybe you'd better tell me the story."

"We learned it last year in Theme. See, there was a great flood that killed everybody. After the water went down, Raven found a gigantic clam shell on the beach." She pantomimed the trickster's discovery, reaching down to pluck up an imaginary clam. "So, of course, he picked it up. And, of course, he looked inside. And inside were all these little, tiny people. So he talked to them, just coaxed and coaxed, until they decided to come out." She ended her lesson with an emphatic nod. "The people inside the clam were the first Haida."

I couldn't resist a little lesson of my own. "Lots of different kinds of people have stories like that. It's called a creation myth, and the one told by your ancestors took place in the Garden of Eden."

"Duh! Adam and Eve, and the apple and all that junk." She threw me an impish grin before skipping ahead, tossing her last words over her shoulder. "I know that, Mom. *Everybody* knows that!"

The distance between us grew as I approached the last house on the shore road, and my daughter disappeared around a bend up ahead just as I passed it. To catch up, I broke into a trot. A few short days before, I'd have continued to stroll unconcerned. Back then, the notion of anyone coming to grief in a Haida village had defied conventional wisdom. But then Sam Houston Larrabee died, and Captain Chaloner's analysis had reminded me that one man's accident could be another man's murder. So I jogged along the shore, Jessie's sports bag flopping against my hips as the shadows deepened in the woods beside the road.

A mist of sweat popped out along my hairline. As I opened my mouth to call out, I found her, still as a statue in the thick grass on the sea side of the road, her eyes fixed on the beach and one hand raised like a traffic cop signaling STOP! Just ahead, the lights of Mission Cottage shone out from the shadows between the trees. And then my left foot made contact with a small rock, launching the pebble off the road and down, down, down, to clatter onto the beach a half-dozen yards below. At the sound, Jessie spun toward me, raising one hand to her lips for quiet while the other waved me forward—slowly.

I eased ahead, stepping lightly and deliberately to

avoid making a sound. When I neared, she reached out behind herself blindly and I gave her my hand. She drew me close, her voice a breathy whisper I could barely hear above the slow wash of the surf. "She's on that rock just offshore; the one that looks like a haystack."

I studied the beach below, a narrow thread of pebbles with a scattering of offshore rocks that shattered the smooth curls of the waves. Crouched just behind the rim of Jessie's haystack rock, a river otter paused her grooming long enough to study us with bright black eyes. To the Maxwell clan, river otters default as females because of the one who lives in the dammed up creek near our home in Eagle River. "She's not as big as Esther."

Jessie nodded her agreement. "But she acts just the same. She's only pretending to wash, just like Esther, but she's got something on that rock with her."

That something turned out to be a three-foot lingcod still gasping in the suffocating atmosphere of our world. After determining that Jessie and I posed no threat to her catch, the otter dragged the green fish out from under herself, braced both webbed front feet against the heaving sides, and tore into the soft underbelly, filling her mouth and bloodying her whiskers before raising her head again to keep us under observation.

"Eeooww! That fish looks like something out of *Jurassic Park.*" Trust my Jess not to recoil at evidence that nature is indeed bloody in tooth and claw. Instead, she leaned forward slightly for a better view and entirely forgot to whisper. "Those puffed out gills make it look kind of like triceratops."

At the sound of her voice, the otter froze for a moment, eyes unblinking and mouth not chewing, as if gauging whether the sudden sound made us more or less likely to try to steal her dinner. After a few seconds, she began to chew again and, when her mouthful disappeared into her gullet, again plunged into the writhing lingcod.

Somewhere behind us, a door closed firmly. "Bet that's Vanessa." I didn't bother to lower my voice, and at this sound the otter didn't even flinch. "Boy, will she be surprised to see you!"

That prediction managed to pry Jessie's eyes from the feasting otter below, and she turned toward Mission Cottage. "Who's that with her?"

The question pried my eyes away. From the shadows around the Cottage, two women had emerged, both of whom I recognized instantly. But before I could answer my daughter, she scooted away, running full-tilt into Vanessa's wide-open arms.

A half step behind Vanessa walked Colleen Malloy, an Anchorage-based FBI agent I'd met at Denali National Park the summer before. Almost a year earlier, we'd parted as friends of a sort after knocking heads more than once in the course of Malloy's investigation of the murder of a visiting Russian scientist. When my daughter bowled into Vanessa, the FBI agent shot me a quick grin. I hurried forward to make introductions and offer Vanessa a hasty explanation of Jessie's presence. At first, Jessie seemed content to cuddle against her Alaska auntie, studying the slim stranger with the dark hair and formidable title from the safety of Vanessa's arms. But after a moment, her curiosity couldn't be contained. She poked her head forward. "Do you have a gun?"

"Yup." Malloy gave her a reassuring smile and opened her jacket wide, revealing the 9mm automatic snugged in a holster under her arm. "But I don't often use it."

Jessie glanced from the gun to Malloy's face and then pulled her head in like a turtle, almost cowering in Vanessa's arms. "My mom shot someone once."

For a moment, no one spoke. Vanessa just tightened her hold on Jessie, and after the searing impact of my daughter's statement, I simply couldn't find words. Colleen Malloy reacted first, dropping to one knee so she could engage Jess on her own level. "I know she did. I was there. Shooting someone is very hard, and your mom was very brave. That was an awful day, but she did the right thing."

From the safety of Vanessa's arms, Jessie listened to the FBI agent's words, eyes solemn and face grave. When Colleen Malloy finished, her gaze rose until her dark eyes met my own and she gave me a dazzling smile. If the FBI said I'd done the right thing, my actions must have been okay. Although I'd never doubted that I'd done the right thing that day in Denali National Park, no one would ever persuade me that shooting someone was okay. Still, I managed to return my daughter's smile, and then Vanessa bundled her off to Mission Cottage, leaving me alone with

Malloy in the gathering twilight. "Thanks, Colleen. I had no idea the shooting still troubled her. I think maybe you finally laid that to rest."

The FBI agent zipped her jacket and turned up the fleece collar. "Kids today get really mixed messages about violence, but police shrinks say affirmation's the key. You did do the right thing, and I'll say that as often as necessary." She tilted her head and shot me a quick glance. "What about your son?"

Jake? My cheeks burned with a sudden flush. How *was* he feeling? I didn't know and admitted as much. "I'm not sure. I guess I'd better find out."

"Remember to call if you need me to talk to him." Malloy didn't give me a chance to thank her again. Instead, she got right down to business. In this case, murder. "I'm investigating the death of Charley Massett, which I understand you witnessed."

"The Haida fisherman?" At her nod, I slid the strap of Jessie's sports bag off my shoulder and eased it to the ground. "I was aboard *Le Mistral* when it happened. But Raoul D'Onofre figured the cause was a buildup of fumes in the bilge. That doesn't sound like a job for the FBI."

"The bureau investigates all deaths at sea." She squared off until we faced each other. "And that was no buildup of fumes. A bomb obliterated Charley Massett's fishing boat." She let that news hang in the air for a second before finally coming to the point. "And Captain Chaloner informs me that you seem suspicious about an earlier death—the drowning of a diver."

I took a deep breath and let it out slowly, playing for time to gather my thoughts and organize my words. A year earlier, I hadn't trusted Malloy, and my distrust had almost produced fatal consequences. But in the aftermath of the Denali disaster, she'd proved herself worthy of my confidence. I wouldn't let her down today. "What did Vanessa tell you?"

Malloy shrugged, her face impassive. "We'd hardly finished exchanging introductions when she spotted you two through the window. She did tell me the diver was her nephew and that you'd been staying with him."

I nodded. "For about ten days. And in that time, Sam went wreck diving twice without incident. Did Captain Chaloner tell you I was aboard his cutter when they found Sam's body?"

Malloy's turn to nod but she didn't say anything, so I continued. "They didn't find a boat. And I'm not sure there's actually a wreck out where Sam was found." I paused, searching for words to add weight to amorphous suspicions. "A couple of things were missing—his weight belt and his knife—and a couple of things didn't fit the accident scenario. For one, the cut on Sam's air hose looks clean—almost surgical. And his buoyancy compensator vest was half-inflated—enough to bring him to the surface but not enough to keep his face out of the water."

Malloy gave me a three-count before replying, her voice carefully neutral. "Is that all?"

"No. When I got back to Mission Cottage that day, I discovered the place had been burglarized. In retrospect, I think Sam's house had actually been searched."

At that piece of information, her eyebrows arched ever so slightly. "You didn't tell Captain Chaloner that?"

Heat rushed to my cheeks. "No. Because another friend of Sam's cleaned the place up before I had a chance to tell anybody. And what I attributed to a search, he attributed to teenage vandals."

She turned away then, staring down at the beach. Through the gathering dusk, I tried to make out the boulder where the otter had dined, but she'd gone and the rising tide had washed the haystack rock clean of the bloody remains, just as the tide had washed the Sukkwan Strait clean of the remains of the Haida fisherman and his boat. I spoke aloud the question that surely bedeviled us both. "Why would anyone want to kill a Haida fisherman?"

"I don't know." Colleen Malloy turned her face from the sea. "Why would anyone want to kill your friend?"

I lifted my shoulders into a shrug. "I don't know. And if Sam's house was searched, I don't know what they were looking for or if they found it."

After promising to keep Malloy informed of any sudden insights into those questions, I walked her to the car she'd parked in the drive beside Mission Cottage. "I'm staying tonight at the boarding house and probably heading back to Anchorage tomorrow afternoon. Call me there if you think of anything."

When the brake lights of Colleen Malloy's car

disappeared around a bend in the road, I climbed the steps onto the porch of Mission Cottage and found Vanessa waiting just outside the front door, her gaze scanning the ground around Sam's house, probing each shadow. "I always figured my first FBI agent would be a man, so you can imagine my surprise when she showed up." However forced, the light tone suggested a welcome return to Vanessa's old self but seemed at odds with her behavior. "Still, I wish she hadn't gone."

I decided to keep things light. "Don't tell me you're swearing off men? She doesn't even seem your type."

Vanessa's next words extinguished any hint of fun. "When there's a strange man lurking in my bushes, anyone carrying a big old gun becomes my type."

13

No one would classify my 9mm Beretta as old, but the automatic definitely fit Vanessa's other criterion—big. At least in terms of firepower. My preferred handgun had been Max's .45 caliber Colt, but after the mess at Denali a year earlier, both that weapon and my .38 caliber Smith and Wesson replacement had been padlocked in the U.S. Attorney's evidence locker. One thing I liked about the 9mm was having fifteen rounds in the magazine, especially after my friend described the fellow she'd spotted outside the house earlier in the day. "Not really young—late thirties, I'd say—but strong and powerfully built." She thrust out her chest and waggled her shoulders in a Schwarzenegger imitation. "Definitely a Haida. And he looked more sad than mean. Kind of brooding, I guess."

I switched Jessie's sports duffel to my other hand.

"Did he say anything? Or do anything that seemed strange?"

"He just stood out there for a while, right beyond the shrubs." Vanessa inclined her head toward the thicket of high bush cranberries that separated the yard from the shore road. "He stood out there staring at me standing in here staring at him standing out there." She shook her head and sighed. "I wasn't scared exactly, but, Lauren, the whole thing seemed mighty strange."

I looked out across the yard, my gaze following the paths of light that streamed from the cottage windows to the shrubs beside the road and then moving beyond the bushes to the sea, where a thick bank of fog and clouds had hidden the evening star. A brooding stranger outside, my little girl inside and rain coming on. The combination raised a shiver along my spine. "How long was he out there?"

Vanessa shrugged. "I don't know, sugar. I'm not sure how long he'd been there before I noticed him. I kept an eye on him for maybe half an hour. Then the phone rang, and when I hung up, he was gone." She slapped a hand against her thigh. "Which reminds me. Your boss called. Said he needs that hook baited and pronto!"

I waved a dismissive hand, mentally shooing away the problem of the orcas, and reached for the knob of the front door. Enough trouble loomed before me right here at home. The orcas would just have to wait. Again.

Before I could open the door, Vanessa put a hand

on my outstretched arm. "Lauren, what's going on here? First came Sam's accident, but you know he didn't tear that air hose, and he wasn't one to panic, either." She hardly paused for an answer. "Then that fishing boat exploded and now the FBI shows up. I want to know what's going on."

After settling my face into a neutral mask, I turned to look her in the eye and answered as honestly as I could. "I don't know what's going on. I'm not convinced Sam's death was an accident. And Colleen Malloy says that Massett's definitely was no accident. But beyond that, I just don't know."

For a few seconds, she didn't move or reply, only searched my face with sober eyes before finally releasing her grip on my arm. "All right, then. Time for us to tend to the living."

Inside Mission Cottage, Jessie had taken up residence in my bed and in my jammies, an old pair of tartan flannels that kept the spring chill away. I stopped on the doorsill, shooting out a hip upon which to prop my hand. "You've got a lot of nerve, peanut. I suppose I'll have to sleep on the floor and bare naked, too!"

She giggled and pulled the covers up until only her dancing eyes showed. "You've got sweats in your drawer." The blanket and comforter muffled her words. "I saw 'em."

I carried her duffel past the bed, made room for her gear beside my own in the bureau drawers, and dug out a ratty old pair of navy sweats. "Ready for bed already?"

A yawn interrupted her nod, and she snuggled down into the pillows. "Uh-huh. But first I've got something for you."

I sat beside her on the bed, and her little hand snaked out from underneath the beige comforter, opening slowly to reveal a small, colorfully striped bag of woven cotton wrapped tightly with a length of white string. I lifted the tiny bag from her palm. "What is it?"

She stifled another yawn. "Open it."

After unwrapping the string, I widened the mouth of the little bag and turned it upside down, spilling the contents onto the thick comforter—six tiny figures of wire and thread, three sporting pants and three wearing full-length skirts. I picked up one tiny female form for closer study. "What are they?"

"Worry people." Jessie sighed, and her eyelids fluttered. "To help you sleep. Nina said you were very worried about the orcas and Vanessa, too, so I bought you some worry people." She closed her eyes and dug her cheek into the pillow. "Just whisper your worries to them and then put their bag under your pillow before you go to sleep." Her words slurred a little and slowed a lot. "They'll take . . . your worries . . . so you . . . can . . . rest."

As her breathing settled into the shallow rhythm of sleep, I brushed my lips across her soft cheek and then studied the tiny figure in my hand. From the looks of the cloth and craftwork, the worry people hailed from Central America, another rainy coast where long ago modern man had confronted contemporary descendants of his ancestral self and preached powerful ideals of Christianity which now mingled uneasily with older, polytheistic beliefs. Before turning off my light and snuggling down beside my daughter, I whispered to the worry people, in obeisance to the old ways, and then I placed my automatic within easy reach in the bedside drawer, in recognition of new realities.

Sometime later that night, the storm blew in from the Gulf of Alaska, roaring over Dall and Sukkwan islands, sweeping across the narrow strait to drench Mission Cottage. Rain hissed through the needles of the Sitka spruce overhead, tapped at the windows and gurgled through the gutters. Jessie slept on without stirring, her feet propped atop my right leg and her head burrowing next to my shoulder. I slipped an arm around her and settled back quietly to listen, searching between the spatters of rain for other sounds—a footfall, a creaking door, another's breathing—but discerning nothing beyond the steady, soothing pulse of the storm.

In the darkness above the bed, I tried to conjure the image of a brooding Haida. Who could he be? And what did he want? The only face that appeared above me belonged to another man, the Haida fisherman named Charley Massett who I had seen murdered, according to Colleen Malloy. Just as Sam Houston Larrabee had been murdered. Both men died in staged accidents in the waters off Hydaburg, but that was all that their deaths had in common. Except, perhaps, for motivation. Find out *why* to find out *who.*

I let my eyes close, blotting out the fisherman's face, and slipped the reins on my mind, allowing thoughts to surface randomly as I relaxed toward sleep. Jake sounded like he was okay. Boyce would have his hook. Owen Stuart expected me at the dock tomorrow. Vanessa seemed better. Raoul D'Onofre might be right about the orcas. Jessie loved the sea. Television hated the rain. Kelsey might come. Konstantin would write.

At the thought of the Russian, my body softened a bit, even as my mind twitched with new energy. Would write a line. Sky blue letters on royal blue lines. Sam's letters. Sam's lines. As the rain beat down upon Mission Cottage, enclosing me in the storm's cocoon of sound, one last thought penetrated, a faint memory of the ratcheting whir of Sam's hard drive. What did Sam write?

Hours later, in the pearl light of a dripping dawn, I crept out of my bed, making sure to tuck the covers around Jessie's shoulders, and then tiptoed down the hall and into Sam's room. Vanessa slept in a wanton sprawl, her red hair streaming across the pillow and one bare foot poking out from underneath the navy spread.

Sinking quietly to my knees in front of Sam's desk, I pushed the power button on the Pentium. The machine came alive, tiny lights flashing above the buttons on the CPU, scrolled text glowing on the screen and inside the occasional whir of the hard drive punctuating the quiet huff of the fan. At the prompt, I keyed in the commands for the file manager, intending to search Sam's directories, but a growl from Vanessa froze my hands. "What in hell are you doing? My God, Lauren, the sun's not up!"

I shot her a quick glance, noting the single cracked eyelid, and turned back to the computer. "Checking my E-mail from Boyce. Just go back to sleep. I'll be very quiet."

When she didn't reply, I figured she'd taken my advice, but before I got a chance to check, a low groan warned me the bear was roused for good. "Like hell I will. You aren't on-line, sugar—any fool can see that. You tell me right now what you're doing in Sam's files."

In the next instant, she rose out of the bed, shawled the navy comforter around her shoulders and crossed the room to tower over me like an avenging goddess. "I mean it, Lauren. You tell me what you're up to right this minute."

The weight in her words warned me that she really did mean it, so I finally told her. All of it. As much as I knew. Which wasn't a lot. And all that I suspected. Meaning I finally came clean about the break-in at Mission Cottage and my suspicion that a search, not a theft, had been the burglar's real intention. Vanessa listened quietly, staring down at me as I crouched on the plank floor, my bare feet chilled in the cool light of dawn. I finished by explaining why I'd kept my suspicions a secret from her. "You seemed so blue. I was afraid for you. I didn't want to add to your burden."

At that last bit, she arched an eyebrow. "You still haven't told me what you're doing in Sam's files."

I rocked back onto my heels. "After the search, Sam's computer was on—I heard the hard drive. And Owen Stuart told me he turned it off when he picked up the place. If the searchers turned on Sam's computer, maybe we can figure out what they were looking for."

Vanessa frowned. "If it's still there. Might be they spent some time hitting the delete key." That possibility literally knocked me over, tilting me off my heels and onto my butt, but Vanessa wasn't fazed. "Of course, wiping memory off a hard drive takes some doing. I might be able to recover anything they erased." A tiny smile tugged at the corner of her mouth. "Could take some doing, but I'd say it's worth a try."

Cracking Sam's computer would take patience and concentration, so Vanessa decided to wait until after Jessie and I left for my scheduled rendezvous and orca tour with Owen Stuart. While I organized foul weather gear and Jessie showered off the grime of yesterday's soccer match, Vanessa rustled up a cowboy breakfast worthy of a true daughter of Texas and even packed our lunch. After we ate, Jessie did the dishes, and I worked the phone, managing to track down Kelsey Kavanaugh at the Sweetland Cafe. "You said Monday's a slow news day. If you can shoot some great footage by midafternoon today, what's the chance of a network picking up your story for tomorrow's broadcasts?"

"Depends on the film. There's great and there's *grrrrrreat.*" I couldn't help grinning at the Tony-the-Tiger allusion. "If you get me *grrrrrreat* footage, I'll get you a network broadcast."

"Deal!" For the first time since the appearance of FBI special agent Colleen Malloy, my heart soared. Not only had I finally told the whole truth to Vanessa, I'd also managed to find a news hook at the perfect time for maximum television exposure. Owen Stuart's loyalty to the orcas would make *grrrrrreat* footage for the evening news. "Make sure to bring lots of film!"

Down at the Hydaburg pier, Owen Stuart greeted the arrival of two unexpected passengers, including one toting a camera, with little enthusiasm. He glanced from the three of us to the Zodiac raft tied up beside him and then to the glassy waters of the strait. Although the wind had blown itself out, a gentle drizzle still fell. I decided to tackle his reluctance head-on. "Is the raft rated for four passengers?"

"Oh, yes." He danced from foot to foot, and lines of worry creased the weathered skin at the corner of his blue eyes. "The actual limit is eight."

I gave the raft a once-over, noting the radio plus receiver on the command console in the center and behind that extra gas tanks showing full, plus the jumble of safety gear and ammo cans tied down beneath a cargo net just in front of the wheel. "And you've got life jackets for all of us? Including a small size for Jessie?"

The worry lines smoothed somewhat. "Life jackets, yes, but I only carry two survival suits."

I turned on my heel, searching the flags bannered from the superstructure of *Le Mistral* and the *Kodiak.* Neither the Frenchman's ship nor the Coast Guard cutter flew signals for bad weather, so I turned back to Owen Stuart.

"Outside of a little liquid sunshine, we've got a good forecast—calm seas and no wind to speak of." I plastered a reassuring smile on my face and made certain my tone of voice came across as reasonable in the extreme. "Of course, it's your call to make, Owen. You're the skipper. But we did hope to see some whales."

From the receiver on the command console came a high-pitched whistle, a chirruping tweet that galvanized my daughter. "Who's that?" She darted to the edge of the pier and fell to her knees on the sturdy gray tube of Owen Stuart's raft. "Is that a whale?" A second whistle tweeted from the receiver. "There's another one! They're talking."

A beatific smile spread across the biologist's face. "I believe that's Q 12 and Q 34—a mother and her son."

Kelsey Kavanaugh raised the camera to her shoulder as he stepped past my daughter to the command console in the middle of his raft to check his receiver. "Looks like they're rounding the headland by transmitter four and moving into Tlevak Strait." Owen Stuart crouched down before Jessie and directed the next question to her alone. "Would you like to meet my orcas?"

Her eyes shone as bright as any star. Too bad Kelsey couldn't get Jess on film for my own video collection. "Would I?" A Christmas morning smile spread across my daughter's face. "Would I ever!"

14

Under the gray, drizzling sky, the sea spread before us like liquid mercury, a smooth expanse, glimmering silver between lush green islands wreathed with wisps of fog, the waters' surface marred only by the wake of Owen Stuart's motorized raft as he steered us toward the Tlevak Strait. Up ahead, a dusting of snow adorned the highest reach of Thunder Mountain, which loomed above Dall Island, the outermost barrier in the Alexander Archipelago, beyond which lay the Gulf of Alaska and the open sea. From my perch beside Kelsey Kavanaugh in the bow of the Zodiac, I listened as the cetacean biologist tutored my daughter, who stood beside him at the wheel, in the finer points of orca taxonomy.

"Orcas are not really whales at all. They are the largest of the dolphins. There are two kinds of orca—

residents and transients—and they are very different. Those you heard were residents from Q pod who live close to shore and eat fish." He lifted one hand from the wheel and gestured broadly to encompass the fiords, straits and bays around Prince of Wales Island. "In a word, here. The transients prey on seals, sea lions, porpoises and whales. Transients are much more of a mystery because they are always on the move, just passing through, and we do not know where they go."

Jessie took a moment to digest the information, standing with feet spread wide on the deck and one hand braced on the command console. Although her yellow rain suit kept her dry and the bulky orange life jacket kept her warm, her cheeks glowed pink from the rush of cool air across her face. "Does a transient ever decide to stay here, or does a resident ever decide to go away?"

The question seemed to surprise Owen Stuart, and the glance he tossed my daughter appeared frankly appraising. "They do not mingle and have not for at least one hundred thousand years. We know, from looking at their tissue in a microscope, that they are genetically different races. Do you know what that means?"

"DNA and all that." Jessie shrugged. "Can you tell them apart without a microscope?"

Now Owen Stuart directed his gaze at me, and his broad smile and raised eyebrows told me that my daughter impressed him, a notion that warmed me no end. "Transients have pointed dorsal fins, and residents' fins are rounded."

Jessie tilted her head and looked up at him. "Can they talk to each other?"

Now Owen Stuart shrugged. "We do not know. Transients are more quiet, and the sounds they make are very different."

A deep frown marred Jessie's face. "Sounds? You mean the orcas aren't talking? The mother and son that we heard—weren't they talking?"

"No, peanut. The whales weren't talking." I leaned toward them, letting the wind whip the short hair around my ears, so Kelsey Kavanaugh could steady her camera from my shoulder to her own. "Just because orcas make sounds doesn't mean that whales can talk to each other. Like many species, whales communicate, but without language, they don't have speech."

As the weight of Kelsey's camera settled on my right shoulder, Jessie scrunched up her forehead in thought. "Just because we don't understand them doesn't mean orcas can't talk, Mom." She raised her face toward the cetacean biologist beside her. "Does it, Dr. Stuart?"

In response, Owen Stuart stuck out his tongue, and Jessie giggled. "There! I did not speak, but I communicated." In the next instant, he let out a loud yelp and grabbed Jessie's arm. My daughter jumped in surprise. "I did not speak then, either, but again I communicated."

Although the biologist spoke to my daughter, he really addressed his words to me. "Humans speak, and therefore humans define intelligent communication as the ability to speak. Seems rather narrow to me, narrow and safe. Because if humans broaden their definition of intelligence to include the many species which clearly communicate, would not that affect how humans allow themselves to treat those species?"

For the first time since leaving Hydaburg, the receiver fixed to the wheel console twittered with whale sounds, a pandemonium of whistles and squeaks that wiped the frown off my daughter's face and raised the hair on my arms. Then came a series of sharp smacks that left Owen Stuart's eyes glittering. "That is a fluke slap, a common gesture in greetings. From the sound of all the commotion, Q pod has run into another resident pod."

Behind me, Kelsey growled under her breath, *"Grrrrrreat* footage. Don't move."

As my daughter craned forward avidly, wide eyes scanning the silver surface of the sea, Owen Stuart leaned down to read the display on the receiver. "Transmitter seven." He raised an arm and pointed to the southwest. "About five minutes from here."

After the biologist steered his raft to a southwest heading, Kelsey Kavanaugh directed a change in my position, asking me to belly flop on the bench and brace my hands on the bow so she could crouch across my legs and steady the camera on my shoulder. When

I'd complied, I found myself with the best view in the house, mostly out of the wind and as near the water as possible. The Zodiac skimmed water as smooth as a mirror, heading toward a gray curtain of rain that hung above the strait at the mouth of a narrow fiord. Just before the raft reached the rain, Owen Stuart eased off the throttle and lowered the volume on the receiver, slowing the Zodiac to an idle and allowing us to drift through the wall of rain. Behind that misty curtain, orcas swam.

Rising from the water like so many black sails, a thicket of dorsal fins swayed gently a mere dozen yards off the raft's bow. Remaining still required every ounce of my strength. One, two, five, eight, eleven dorsal fins! And then, so close that I could almost reach out to touch glistening black skin, two more fins rose from the undersea world, and—*kwhoof*—a cloud of vapor erupted from the orcas, immersing me in the oily, fish breath of whales. The nearest one rolled slightly, revealing a belly and chin of brilliant white, and surveyed me with one very brown, very inquisitive eye. The orca lifted a paddle-shaped pectoral fluke from the sea, and water streamed across the glossy black surface. Then the whale rolled again, slapping the fluke against the water and raising a salty splash that left me dripping. And grinning.

"Mama!" Jessie ignored the camera braced on my right shoulder and wiggled along my left side toward the bow of the raft. "He wants to play."

She leaned over the bow, reaching for the water. I grabbed the belt on her life jacket and a handful of her rain pants as she snaked forward, hanging from her hips, to dip both hands in the sea.

"Shit!" Kelsey breathed in my ear. The camera lifted from my shoulder. "This is *grrrrrreat* stuff!"

Jessie scooped the water like a joyous toddler, digging handful after handful to toss at the orcas. More whales surfaced, another half dozen, and the orcas lolled in the water, the whoosh of their breathing a rhythmic counterpoint to my daughter's squeals. The orca nearest the raft sank beneath the glistening surface, vanishing from our world, but in a moment he returned to skyhop, lifting his whole head from the water. A long strand of eel grass trailed from the perpetual grin of his mouth. Jessie snaked forward again, arms outstretched, straining to reach the orca, to touch the magic of another world. But before she could, Owen Stuart knelt beside me on the bow bench and, with one careful heave, gently lifted my daughter back into the raft. "You cannot play with him. Orcas do not exist for human amusement. They are the rulers of the deep and arguably the most evolved intelligence on this planet."

Jessie twisted out of his grasp. "He wouldn't hurt me."

"Not intentionally, perhaps, but orcas have hurt humans." The biologist sat back on his heels. "A trainer at a Canadian aquarium slipped into a tank and the whales drowned her. Perhaps they did not understand that she could not dive for minutes at a time." He smiled to soften his words and gently touched my daughter's arm. "A surfboarder in California required more than a hundred stitches after an orca bit him. Perhaps, from under the water, his silhouette looked like that of a seal."

I settled back along the starboard side of the Zodiac, leaving the bow to teacher and pupil, and Kelsey took up position behind the command console, using the steady center of the raft to anchor her camera. Within the confines of the fiord's towering spruce-covered arms, the sea hardly swelled, seeming slack in the sheltering cove. Only the barest trace of air moved, and even that bore a warm kiss, heavily scented with the fishy breath of the orcas.

Jessie's eyes went dreamy for a moment, and she repeated the biologist's words as one declaims an incantation. " 'They rule the deep.' " Her gaze moved back to the whales lolling in the fiord. "Who is their ruler?"

Owen Stuart's smile widened. "Q 12 is the matriarch of her pod. I have known her for twenty years, and my research indicates that her maternal group is the basis of Q pod." He got to his feet and scanned the resting pods, finally pointing to the orca floating farthest from the raft. "There she is. Do you see the white saddle behind her fin? Each is unique, and hers has a double notch." He gestured his hand toward the rest of the whales. "And many of the orcas here are her family—sons and daughters, brothers and sisters, uncles and aunts. They have their own special dialect, and they always stay together."

Jessie's eyes went round. "Forever?"

"Yes, forever." A frown flitted across his face. "Unless an orca is captured, he lives with his family all of his life. Perhaps fifty years for a male, and as long as seventy for a female. Twenty-five years ago, Q 12's first son was captured. He is in Japan now."

A troubled weight settled upon my daughter's brow, and she rose onto her knees, eyes focused on the bereft mother. In the momentary silence, Kelsey's camera whirred, recording the biologist's lamentation which would provide our desperately needed news hook, but I felt no triumph. My heart ached for my little girl, who knew far more than any child should about losing a loved one. "Do you think she still misses him?"

Owen Stuart's lip curled. "Would you miss your mother if someone snatched you away?"

The biologist's words stabbed through me, robbing me of breath, but Jessie remained composed, giving him a tentative nod. "But orcas aren't people."

"No, orcas aren't people. But you have heard them communicate, have you not? There is Q 34—you heard him, an adolescent male. He'll never leave his mother." Time and again, he jabbed a finger at the floating orcas. "And Q 26—his sister. And Q 16—his aunt. And Q 19—his uncle. Have you ever seen a human family as close as this one?"

Owen Stuart didn't wait for an answer. "These are intelligent creatures, far more intelligent than man. They hunt in packs, just like wolves, and can bring down a blue whale, the largest living thing on earth. They have been photographed taking a polar bear off an ice floe and a moose off a beach! But they rule their world with far more intelligence than man rules his."

"They're awfully brave and strong." Her nose wrinkled in thought. "But how are they smarter than people?"

"Orcas do not make war." He glanced down at her, an eyebrow arched in appraisal. "They kill for food, only as much as they need, and they never kill each other. Instead they band together for life, take care of each other's offspring, and never harm another of their species. Can the same be said of man?"

For a moment, no one spoke. The biologist's words seemed perfect for the *grrrrr*eat footage, and apparently Kelsey Kavanaugh agreed. "Gotta move, people." She spoke with a new urgency but kept her camera at the ready. "Gotta feed this film to the network as soon as possible."

Without another word, Owen Stuart moved back to his command console, and Kelsey stepped aside to give him room. Jessie leaned over to brush a kiss against my cheek and whisper in my ear, "I think Owen likes the orcas more than he likes people."

"So whaddya think, Jess?" Kelsey crouched until the camera reached my daughter's level, and a playful tone of self-mockery rang behind her words. "What's your opinion of the proposed capture of twelve orcas?"

With the clear vision and unwavering certainty that only youth possesses, my daughter looked straight into the camera's lens and spoke the words that none of us would soon forget. "Putting a whale in a tank is just plain mean."

15

WHAT MOTHER COULD FORGET THE WORDS THAT made her daughter an instant celebrity? Not that I had any premonition of impending doom when Jessie addressed Kelsey's camera and, as it turned out, the entire world. After Owen Stuart piloted his raft back to Hydaburg, we returned to Mission Cottage in early afternoon to find Vanessa still chained to Sam's Pentium, systematically rescuing deleted files through a procedure I couldn't fathom. Which wasn't surprising since I still had trouble with Microsoft's undelete application. While she slaved in the bedroom, Jessie and I spent the rest of a very rainy day in the kitchen making cookies, from-scratch brownies and dough for the pepperoni pizza my daughter had requested for dinner. Vanessa joined us for the meal, explaining that actually reading Sam's files would have to wait until everything recoverable had been salvaged, lest we do further damage. I asked about the condition of his diskettes, and Vanessa had a quick and definitive answer: "There aren't any. Not even blanks. I had to open that new box from the case of your laptop." No disks? That shut me up, at least until Jessie went to bed. Except that after snuggling with my daughter while she read out loud a chapter from her latest book and then whispering my concerns to the worry people, I conked out, too.

Much, much later, as the first faint glimmers of dawn tinted the stormy sky, I woke to find Vanessa hissing in an irritated whisper and brandishing Sam's portable phone. "It's your boss, for God's sake. And he just ordered me to turn on the damned TV!"

"Huh!"

Apparently that eloquent reply provided all the clues Boyce Reade needed to conclude that I had taken the phone. By the time the receiver reached my ear, he'd raced past a greeting and on into enthusiastic praise. "—brilliant, Lauren, just brilliant! Do you have the right channel? The teaser should be on in less than a minute."

A blare of static erupted from the living room, followed quickly by Vanessa's furious snarl, "Are you coming? It's not my job on the line!"

However exaggerated her assertion, even the remote possibility of unemployment spurred me out of the cozy bed where my daughter still slept and on across the entry hall to the living room where the television glowed in the fast-fading twilight of Alaska's brief spring dawn. Although I'm not much for

TV, I recognized the strains of the theme music of network television's most popular morning show. And as I sank onto the couch beside Vanessa, I also recognized the giggling girl on the screen who scooped handfuls of water out of a silver sea. My heart had frozen in my chest long before she turned to face the camera with solemn brown eyes and emphatically declared, "Putting a whale in a tank is just plain mean."

"Shit!" The word groaned out of me.

"That's Jess!" Vanessa squealed with delight.

"And she's fabulous!" Boyce's enthusiasm held the exultation of an answered prayer.

As if on cue, a quick tattoo of footsteps danced across the front porch, followed immediately by an eager knocking on the front door. Vanessa's grin faded. "Who could that be? At this hour?"

Who else? She started to get up, but I grabbed her arm and held her down. "Don't answer it!"

Vanessa flinched. "You don't think it's him?"

For a moment, I hadn't a clue who she was talking about. Then I remembered the Haida she'd seen lurking in the bushes and shook my head. "Not him. Them!" I jerked a thumb at the television. "The media!"

Bang, *bang, BANG!* Another flurry of knocks rattled the hinges on the front door. Then a voice floated into the room as an insistent hand jiggled the locked handle. "Hello? Anybody home?"

Vanessa and I remained on the couch, each of us holding our breath and ignoring the squawks from the portable phone in my lap, frozen like two conspirators caught in the act of some dreadful deed as a pert television blonde chirped out the morning's news. And then America's latest celebrity child emerged from the bedroom.

"Mama?" Jessie stood in the hall, one hand scratching her head, and blinked the sleep from her eyes. "Why aren't you answering the door?"

"Vanessa's just getting it, sweetie. You come on over and sit with me on the couch." I gently dug my nails into my friend's arm and spoke in a hush. "Do not open the door. Do not let anyone in."

While Jessie padded across the floor, I raised the telephone to my ear. She curled up beside me and rested her head on the armrest while I told my boss a terrible truth. "This is a disaster."

"No, it's not!" A thread of outrage wove through the smooth texture of his voice. "It's terrific! You have no idea!"

I cut him off. "From a parent's point of view, this *is* a disaster." Undelete and retakes are the province of the one who owns the technology. Which left whining my only recourse, and I am not a whiner. "But it's done and can't be undone. So tell me how it looks from Wild America's point of view?"

"Terrific! Beyond belief!" His voice chimed with triumph. "The phones ring nonstop, the fax is churning out page after page, and Sally says the E-mail's piling up at an amazing rate! If the same thing's happening at the White House—and it *has* to be—we may have turned the corner. The way this thing looks from here, your daughter just may have saved the whales! At the very least, she's got everybody's attention."

Out in the hallway, Vanessa had apparently ignored my advice about keeping the door closed. How like a Texan to expect common courtesy even from a mob of television types! For a moment, I tuned out Boyce and tuned in Vanessa. From the sounds of things, her attitude had moved straight past cantankerous and on to irate, rising in volume all the while. "I'm fixing to bite that arm if you don't take it out of my door." A yelp of pain followed her warning. "Your leg isn't broke, mister, but it will be if you don't vacate these premises now." A note of outraged authority rang out with her words. "That goes for all you varmints. Vamoose!" A grunt of exertion followed, and then the door clunked against the jamb and the dead bolt snapped into place.

"Lauren? Are you still there?"

I glanced from my daughter, who stared wide-eyed at the television screen where her own image suddenly hung behind the blond newscaster's shoulder, to Vanessa, whose eyes sparkled with anger, and made the only sensible decision. "Boyce? Let me call you back. Things are going crazy here!" Before he could protest, I stabbed the button to disconnect and prepared for the second wave of outrage and excitement.

"Mama!" Jessie leaped from the couch and ran to the television, standing before it in wonder. "Mama, that's me! That's yesterday!"

"Of all the nerve." Vanessa plopped onto the couch

beside me, clenching and unclenching the fists that lay in her lap. "They tried to barge right in here. No matter that I said, 'No, we weren't ready for company.' On they came!" A malicious glitter flashed through her eyes. "I wish I had broken that fool's leg!"

Before I could reply, the phone I still held in my hand trilled urgently. Despite the insistent peel, I considered just not answering, but then shushes erupted from the woman steaming beside me and the child transfixed before me, so I barked into the mouthpiece, "Hello?"

"Most mothers would love to see their kid on network television." At least Kelsey Kavanaugh had the guts to lead with her chin. "But, then, I figured you weren't any ordinary mother."

I propped the phone between shoulder and ear, and relaxed against the couch. "Is that an apology?"

"Do you want one?"

I sighed and gave up all thoughts of retribution. "I'll settle for an explanation."

"The producer in New York made the call after previewing the footage, and apparently the decision wasn't even close. I found out just before midnight and decided to let you get one last good night's sleep before hell broke loose."

On the television screen, Kelsey's footage of my daughter segued from shot to shot—at the wheel of the Zodiac, hanging over the bow of the raft, listening attentively to Owen Stuart's lesson in cetacean biology and announcing her earnest opinion to a cynical world—while the newswoman provided a telephoned play-by-play in my ear. "She looks so sturdy standing there. And so spunky trying to play with those huge creatures! Talk about smart—everybody can see that even a world-class scientist's impressed. Which just adds weight to her words." Kelsey couldn't keep pride from infecting her voice. "Whaddya bet 'Just plain mean' becomes this year's 'Where's the beef?' "

"I've got the beef! Shit, do I ever." Jess tossed me a questioning glance, so I threw her a smile in return and rose from the couch, walking back toward the entry hall. "Not that I mind looking like a careerist fanatic who'd sacrifice her own daughter to the cause. Kind of like the enviro equivalent of Chuck Colson, don't you think?"

From her end of the phone, Kelsey drew a sharp breath but didn't interrupt my tirade. "But guess what happens if Raoul D'Onofre succeeds in taking twelve orcas? If that happens—*when that happens*—my daughter fails."

I stepped into the entry and turned toward the front door, keeping my voice low even as I moved out of my daughter's hearing range. "In front of the whole fucking world, Jessie Maxwell takes a huge fucking fall. Which translates into kidthink as, 'It's all my fault.' So you TV types have all the fun you want hyping the hell out of my little girl today, but remember that after that damned Frenchman grabs the orcas, I'll be the one trying to put Jessie Maxwell back together again."

On the other end of the phone line, Kelsey Kavanaugh groaned. "Oh, God, I never thought of that!

I'm so sorry! Your poor little girl! This could ruin her life!"

Well, not really. Kelsey's youthful hyperbole managed to snap me back to reality. From my own more mature perspective, the immediate need became damage control. If I could insulate Jess from the video hounds baying outside our door, perhaps I could minimize the disaster and maybe even spare her from a ruined life. Ignoring the muted apologies, I did my best to snap Kelsey out of it, too. "Get a grip, kid. I need some information."

"Like what?"

"Like how long are these TV guys going to pester us?" I glanced through the single pane of glass on the front door and noted that the news hounds—all two, four, seven, nine of them—had retreated to the street, where they huddled in a miserable knot in a sudden downpour. When had it started to rain? "They actually tried to force their way inside a minute ago."

"Don't open the door!" I couldn't resist a grin when Kelsey echoed my earlier warning to Vanessa. "They'll stay all day at least and maybe all night, too."

"Even in a drenching rain?"

"In any kind of weather. They've got producers yelling at them to get an interview with Jessie, and they'll stay as long as their producers tell them to."

I peeked out again through the window in the front door. A couple of fellows had climbed into the cab of a battered pickup parked across the road, several tried to squeeze under the canopy of a single umbrella and another pair held a blue plastic utility tarp tented above their heads. At least with the press mob outside our door, we didn't have to worry too much about the Haida man who'd spooked Vanessa two days earlier. And with that kind of rain, even my web-footed daughter would be happy to curl up inside Mission Cottage for a quiet day. Which would give me a great opportunity to peruse Sam Houston Larrabee's undeleted files.

I turned my attention back to Kelsey. "What about the phone?"

"May as well leave it off the hook. Otherwise they'll just drive you batty." Her voice brightened. "Hey, didn't you say you were on-line? At least you won't be completely cut off."

"Thank God for E-mail." I dug down deep and summoned up what little graciousness remained within me. "And thanks for helping me out with this, Kelsey. It's not your fault."

"But what about Jessie? What if the hunters do get their permits to take orcas? What happens then? What'll you do?"

For the first time since Vanessa had shaken me awake less than an hour earlier, Kelsey's questions forced me to face the changed circumstances that now confronted me. The effort to save the orcas had always been personal because my mistake had first placed them in harm's way. But now the stakes were much, much higher and way more personal. Now my daughter was in harm's way, too. Funny how threats to one's children can launch a parent off the fence and convert a committed peacemaker into a wild-eyed warmonger.

"Do?" I gripped the telephone tightly and glanced once more at the miserable fellows huddled outside in the rain. "Whatever it takes to stop them, that's what I'll do."

16

CABIN FEVER IS NOT A SYNDROME THAT'S UNIQUE to Alaskans, but the Great Land may endure a particularly virulent strain of the affliction. The discomfort can be especially tough on those who've already survived months of cold darkness only to find themselves trapped inside by nasty weather on an otherwise lighted day. Of the three of us who shared the shelter of Mission Cottage that soggy spring day, by far the worst afflicted was my daughter. I managed to occupy her all morning by losing every game of cribbage and gin that we played, all the while wondering why I'd never taken her to Vegas. After lunch, Jessie consented to curl up on my bed with a good book, but when I went in a half an hour later to retrieve my laptop, I found her kneeling at the window, chin propped on the sill, and staring out at the endless ranks of breakers rolling toward the beach. I dropped into a crouch behind her and enfolded her in my arms. "Looks like that rain doesn't bother you at all. I bet you'd much rather be out there running on the beach."

She leaned against me. "Why don't I just go out and talk to those men, Mama? If I did that, wouldn't they leave us alone?"

Rather than replay my earlier explanation of her captivity, I offered her a chance to make a choice. "Why don't you go look through Sam's movies? There's lots of them."

She sighed heavily. "Probably dumb old grown-up movies."

"Some of them are." I snuggled my face into the sweet spot under her ear. "But just like your dad, Sam loved John Wayne. I'm sure there's something in there you haven't seen."

Always eager to reestablish the connection to the father she hardly remembered, Jessie scampered off to sift through Sam's video collection, which towered all around the television, and I carried my laptop into his bedroom. Despite my eagerness to plunge into the reading of Sam's salvaged files, Vanessa put me off. "I've recovered everything, including lots of junk. Give me a couple of hours to make some sense of it all."

While she occupied herself through the afternoon with identifying and sorting the files she'd recovered from Sam's hard drive, I went on-line and exchanged a flurry of E-mail with my boss, who'd worked late in order to gauge and milk the reaction to Jessie's appearance on the morning news, and with my son, who couldn't believe his sister was now a global personality, and didn't bother pretending to like taking her messages. "Don't even try to call," Jake finally wrote. "We turned off the fax and phone. These people are stupid, Mom. No one believes us when we say you're not here. How could you be here and Hydaburg at the same time? Nina says I can stay with Jared till this is over. Tell Jessie thanks a lot. No, tell her she did good. She did, didn't she, Mom?"

If my boss's reaction was any indication, Jess did more than good—she did great! When the day's last edition of the *New York Daily News* hit the streets with "Just plain mean" bannered in huge type above a picture of Jess reaching toward the orca, Boyce was ready to declare victory.

"The NYDN clinches it," he wrote. "This is not an issue of elites or of bleeding heart liberals. Opposition cuts across political, regional, economic and demographic lines. Jessie's framed the issue in exactly the kind of human terms that anybody can understand. When does she next meet the press?"

For a long moment, I stared at the question glowing on the screen of the laptop propped on the bed before me. I'd unplugged Sam's Pentium from the phone jack and connected my computer instead, and the short wire didn't give me much room to range. An arm's length away, Vanessa toiled at Sam's keyboard, fingers clattering across the keys to work her magic with the files. After considering and rejecting a half dozen more diplomatic replies, I keyed in my answer—"Jessie will not be meeting the press again"—and hit the send key, zapping the message on its way to our nation's capital. Then, after zapping one last E-mail to Jake at his friend Jared's E-mail address, I logged off the Internet and, just for good measure, pulled the plug from the phone jack.

"Ride, boldly ride!" My daughter twirled through the door. "A gallant knight, in sunshine and in shadow." Jessie struck a pose, one hand on her hip and the other raised with a finger pointing toward heaven. "He journeyed long, singing a song, in search of El Dorado." She swept her hand high. "Over the mountains of the moon." She swept her hand low. "Down the valley of the shadow." And then she clasped her hands together as if in prayer. "Ride, boldly ride!"

At her first words, Vanessa had spun her chair around to face my daughter. Now she arched an eyebrow in her direction. "Sounds like you've made the acquaintance of Alan Badillion Trahern."

At her observation, Jessie nodded happily and twirled back out the door. My turn to arch an eyebrow. "Explanation?"

"*El Dorado*—one of Duke's more forgettable pictures." She shrugged. "But it *is* about Texas." She spun back to the desk. "Scoot over here so you can see the screen. I'm just about finished with Sam's files."

Vanessa started my tour in the file cabinet, keying in the command to read the disk in the A drive. "I've sorted all Sam's files into different folders. A lot of it was junk—temporary files from his word processor, remnants of old programs, stuff like that—but three kinds of files turned out to be keepers."

She moved the mouse until the on-screen arrow pointed to a graphic of a file folder labeled LETTERS. "First, his correspondence." The arrow moved down to a file folder labeled DATA. "And a bunch of research files—interviews, reading notes, things of that kind." The arrow dropped to the last folder, which bore the label BOOK. "This is an outline and a bunch of chapters."

She double-clicked and double-clicked again, summoning a text file to the screen. I read the title page out loud. *"People of the Misty Isles: A Sojourn Among the Haida.* By Sam Houston Larrabee." A fierce pain stabbed through me. "A book! They deleted Sam's book?"

Vanessa lifted her chin, eyes brimming with unshed tears. "I got it back."

She double-clicked again, and the left side of the screen filled with a long row of file names, each beginning with the same letters: CHAPTR. There were a dozen in all. "That's his life's work, Lauren. And we almost lost it. If Sam made a hard copy and backup disks—and I'm sure he did—they took those as well."

That observation eased the pain in my chest. "So now we know what was taken." I put my hand on her shoulder and squeezed. "Don't you see? The rest of it—the huge mess they made—was all for show. To distract us from this." I flicked a fingernail against the screen of Sam's computer. "Somewhere in those files is a motive for murder."

Vanessa grabbed a blue disk from the desk and offered it to me. "I'll take his correspondence, you take his research notes. Got a suggestion for a search term?"

I took the disk she offered. "Dive. Diving. Wreck. Wreck diving," she replied with a frown, so I explained my reasoning. "For starters, let's fill in the gaps in the knowns. Sam died diving. I want to know where he'd been diving. And with whom."

Thank God for software! Finding every instance of those words in Sam's research files proved effortless—the computer performed the heavy labor. I merely inserted the disk into my laptop, opened a file, keyed in the word *dive* and waited the fraction of a millisecond it took the machine to locate that word in the text. Not that all of Sam's files contained the word *dive.* In fact, most didn't. So first I sorted, moving files that contained the word into a new folder I titled DIVE.

When a tiny choked sob escaped Vanessa, I leaned toward my friend. "What have you got?"

"Just a letter to me." She blotted her eyes with the hem of her T-shirt and gave me a trembling smile. "I've got to quit reading everything I find and just look for his damned diving log."

I moved back to my own workstation on the bed. After isolating Sam's diving files, I started reading, rapidly scanning the text for clues to the locations of his dives and his companions. Painstaking as he was, Sam Houston Larrabee made things easy for me by keeping three kinds of diving files: a simple log listing each dive's date and time, location expressed in latitude and longitude, and water and sea conditions; a cross-referenced inventory of objects recovered; and a brief narrative summary of each dive, including a description of underwater terrain and the condition and origin of any wreck that he found. From the looks of things, he'd dived alone, systematically searched the waters around Hydaburg for historic wrecks and made sure every object he'd found wound up in the possession of tribal authorities. My heart soared when I discovered that the last entry in the log was dated the day of Sam's death. But that flight proved short-lived because Sam's final entry trailed off into a nonsensical garble of letters and symbols.

I placed my laptop on the edge of the bed, screen facing out. "Vanessa, look at this."

She spun away from the desk and rolled up to the bed. "That's garbage. So what?"

"Was it always garbage?" I hit the page up key, so she could see an intact portion of Sam's dive log. "Or did the real data get scrambled?"

Line by line, she scrolled down until the garbage at the end of Sam's log reappeared on the screen. "Probably the real data got scrambled. What do you think it was?"

I scrolled just enough text to reveal one intact entry. "Based on what precedes it, I'd guess that garbage used to specify the location of Sam's last dive." I gave her a two-count to let the significance of that statement sink in. "Any chance of recovering the data?"

After a moment, she sighed heavily. "No way. Looks like that sector was written over sometime after the original file was deleted. Writing over permanently wipes out the original." She raised bleak eyes to meet my own. "This won't work, Lauren. We don't even know what we're looking for."

Fulfilling the old adage that misery loves company, my daughter appeared in the bedroom doorway to add a whine of her own. "Can't we go out now?" She walked to the window. "They'll never see us in this fog."

I joined her there. While we'd been otherwise occupied, a thick bank of fog had rolled over Mission Cottage, smothering the last of the day's light and wrapping the house in dense gray layers of mist. Outside, droplets of water trickled down the window glass, and visibility appeared reduced to mere feet. Inside the tension built inexorably. Jessie did need an outing. And even if the TV types momentarily saw us as we rolled by in Sam's Land Cruiser, they probably wouldn't be able to find us again. I could either run that risk, or I could sit tight and spend the rest of the evening closeted with two very mopey ladies of my acquaintance. Talk about cabin fever! Turned out the call wasn't even close!

In the Toyota parked beside the house, the fog had slithered moist fingers through tiny cracks, leaving the steering wheel clammy under my hands and the ignition skittish at my first attempt to start the engine.

"Shit!" In the roomy seat behind me, Vanessa had huddled Jessie on the floor out of sight, and a nervous squeal escaped my daughter at that fitful grinding. But the fog had dulled all the sensory edges of the world, muffling the steady rhythm of the sea and the angry growl of the Toyota. When I tried again, the engine caught immediately. "Hang on!"

I flipped on the headlights and wheeled into reverse, backing quickly, turning sharply and praying fervently that no one and nothing lay in my way. A bit too sharp on the turn, and in the brief time I took to correct that mistake, something loomed before me, a ghostly hunchback trapped between the beams of the headlights, the misshapen silhouette of a man shouldering an unwieldy camera. When I leaned on the horn and stomped on the accelerator, the cameraman leaped aside. "We're outta here!"

Around the next bend in the road, the first homes appeared, windows glowing dully in the fog with the cold light of a dying sun. I cracked the window to listen for the sound of an engine behind us. Nothing. The Toyota's motion drew in several strands of smoke, scents of burning spruce and cedar that curled out of the town's chimneys and slid to the ground under the weight of the fog. The tang of the sea also flavored the smoky stew, and along the docks, the lights of the boats and ships rocked on the waves, faintly twinkling like distant stars.

Jessie bounced on the seat behind me, entranced by a shadowed world sculpted by fog. "Mama, let's walk! Can we walk?"

After parking the Toyota in the tiny lot near the Sweetland Cafe, I locked arms with Jessie and Vanessa and steered them away from the restaurant, heading for the strictly residential side streets. But up ahead a door banged open, spilling an oblong of light, and three amorphous forms emerged from Hydaburg's venerable boarding house. Reporters! Had to be, since the press had commandeered every spare bed in town! And we were trapped between them and their probable destination—Sweetland! When in fact the trio started in our direction, I swung my companions toward the next building and ducked through the door.

Poised directly across from us, between a pair of carved house posts at the head of the spacious room, a grizzled Haida man stood with arms spread wide, displaying a ceremonial robe fashioned of cloth that depicted a red double-headed eagle sewn onto a field of black and outlined with a double-row of pearl buttons. Jessie freed her arm from my grasp and pointed. "Oohh, a button-blanket. Isn't it pretty, Mama?"

Her question dropped into a momentary hush in the Hydaburg village hall like a pebble tossed into a quiet pool. And like the ever-widening ring that the pebble creates, Jessie's words inspired a subtle but distinct movement as one by one, from their seats on the built-in bench that circled the perimeter of the village hall, the elders of Hydaburg sent quick, shy glances in our direction. My cheeks flamed with sudden heat, but before I could stumble back outside, dragging my companions with me, Vanessa inclined her head first to the left and then to the right, and gently guided me to a seat on the nearest bench. Jessie trailed behind and flopped down beside me, leaning her head against my shoulder. I threw an arm around my daughter, plastered a pleasant smile on my face and did my best to whisper between clenched teeth, "I'm not sure what we interrupted, but I don't think we should stay."

Vanessa whispered right back through her own phony smile. "We have to." She placed her hand on my knee, index finger rigid against the denim of my jeans. "See that fellow across the room? The one with the old lady?"

Oh-so-casually, I allowed my eyes to drift around the circle of faces until I encountered the frank gaze of a thirty-something man who sat beside a tiny woman who held a large bentwood box in her lap. "The one who's staring at us?"

"Staring at me staring at him. That's the one." She tightened her grip on my knee. "That's the man I saw lurking in the bushes."

17

The brooding weight of the lurking Haida's eyes settled on me with the icy touch of the fog that swirled outside the Hydaburg village hall. I tightened my grip on my daughter's shoulders. I didn't know him. I didn't even recognize him. Which meant that during my short stay in Hydaburg, we probably hadn't crossed paths. And since Vanessa's stay had been that much shorter and more closely confined to Mission Cottage, the possibility that the brooding Haida knew her seemed equally unlikely. So the only thing that could have drawn him to Mission Cottage was the house itself. Or what that house contained.

"Look at this robe." The grizzled elder at the front of the hall spoke with quiet authority. "Show me the evil in this button blanket."

When the elder made that demand, the brooding Haida turned his attention back to the meeting we'd interrupted. A robust woman stepped forward, a large black book clenched in one hand and a gold six-pointed star adorning the front of her long blue tunic. "The Bible says we must renounce the hidden works of darkness."

Under my hand, Jessie's shoulder stiffened and she straightened up, intent on the confrontation unfolding before us. Thank God she'd decided to reserve her questions until after the action finished.

The preacher lifted her Bible above her head. "There will be no button blankets in heaven. You won't need them there. You don't need anything besides Jesus. That's why God told me we must burn these evil idols."

Between the lurking Haida across the way and the conflict playing out in the center of the hall, I hadn't noticed the approach of a wizened Haida elder. Now he stopped before Vanessa to murmur a few words of condolence for Sam's death. Behind him came another Hydaburg elder and then another, a trickle building into a steady, quiet stream of villagers taking advantage of the unexpected opportunity to pay their respects. And from the look on my friend's face, a bittersweet mixture of joy and sorrow, their gesture would deliver the expected therapeutic payoff. As I'd learned in my own experience of grief, such outpourings of affection help the healing.

At the front of the hall, a young man sporting a Mariner's ball cap displayed a miniature totem carved in argillite. "This is the work of the devil, and

Jesus calls on us to renounce the work of the devil. To be saved, we must burn the past. This I will burn."

Jessie turned to say something to me, but before she could, a shout erupted. "No!" A twenty-something woman leaped to her feet, setting off a musical chime from the carved gold bracelets that decorated both wrists. "That totem is not yours to burn. And that button blanket doesn't belong to Joe Skidegate, either. Such treasures belong to all of us—all the *Haada*—and you hold them now just for safekeeping."

She took a step forward, arms spread wide. "Don't you see? You can't destroy your past without harming mine. More than a century ago, when the missionaries first came, the people cut their totems and sold their treasures, except for these few. Our past was carted away to Seattle and New York and Washington, except for these few. Let us not make the same mistake again."

Silence followed the young woman's plea, marred only by the quiet footsteps of those villagers still offering their condolences to Vanessa. No one stood to speak, and most of the villagers seated on the bench that circled the hall seemed lost in thought. Even my daughter joined in their silent deliberations, shifting her gaze between each of the Haida who'd spoken—Joe Skidegate, the preacher, the Mariner fan and the impassioned young woman—as if weighing their conflicting arguments. Then the frail woman beside the brooding Haida rose to her feet, the large bentwood box balanced in her hands. "I will show you evil."

That got Jessie's attention. She sidled a bit closer to me and slid her arm through mine.

The old woman gestured for her younger companion to take the box, and when he did, she opened the lid and withdrew her treasure, an ancient ceremonial mask of beaten silver, intricately hammered and carved to depict a grinning orca. "Here is evil."

With trembling fingers, the frail woman held the stunning mask before her and turned slowly, displaying the orca's grin to every corner of the room. "Once, long ago, the people brought this metal from the sea but in return the *Haada* lost their great chief. So the elders of the clan built the silver blackfish a special box to hold him and entrusted the safeguarding of the evil spirit to the great chief's wife."

Despite the ominous promise of revealed evil, my daughter leaned forward to study the grinning mask. Cedar, gold and argillite—those were the Haida's preferred media. I couldn't remember ever before seeing a Haida object worked in silver. Nor had I ever heard of silver mined from the sea.

The old woman returned the mask to the carved wooden box and firmly closed the lid. "From that time until this, from mother to daughter and grandmother to granddaughter, none spoke of the silver blackfish and the evil spirit was contained. But then I spoke and the evil escaped, killing one man and then another, a white man first and then one of our own."

Beside me, Jess gasped, and I'll confess to experiencing that weird sensation when the hair on one's arms actually stiffens and salutes. A white man! Was she talking about Sam Houston Larrabee? And then one of their own. She had to mean the Haida fisherman, Charley Massett! All at once her cryptic tale of an evil silver blackfish took on new importance. After all, she'd as much as admitted that something she said got both men killed.

Taking the box from the brooding Haida's hands, she carried it to the center of the hall and placed it on the floor. "Here is evil. If you would destroy evil, then begin with this."

Like a magnet of enormous, irresistible power, the carved box drew the people of Hydaburg. From one side of the room came the girl with the golden bangles, and from the other side came the young baseball fan. The preacher clutched the Bible to her chest and advanced toward the carved box slowly, but Joe Skidegate set aside the folded button blanket before trotting forward to grab the box. As the other elders streamed across the floor, the preacher raised her Bible and her voice. But new voices rose to confront hers, and the sound of their fear and their hope swelled to fill the room, growing from the gentle breezes of concerned whispers to the violent gusts of angry shouts as the knot of people surrounding the box grew into a crowd and then into a mob.

On one side of me, Jessie slipped her hand into my own. "Mama, why is everybody so mad all of a sudden?"

And on the other, Vanessa grabbed my arm. "What did she mean about Sam? I don't understand. We've got to talk to that woman."

My thoughts exactly, but as the pandemonium built in the village hall, monopolizing our attention, the old woman vanished, along with her brooding companion. As soon as Vanessa figured that out, she spun toward the door, and Jessie and I followed her back into the fog. Outside the village hall everything had changed. An hour before, the mist had appeared white and clean, but now a sickly yellow tinged the smoky stew. The sweet fragrance of burning cedar had been replaced by the bitter odor of dying ashes. We huddled together in the empty street, and I wondered how the fantastic unreality of our magical adventure had metamorphosed into the vague spookiness of an eerie dream.

When we approached the small parking lot beside the darkened Sweetland Cafe, Sam's Land Cruiser loomed out of the mist, listing sharply to one side like a sinking ship. With my pocket flashlight, I traced over the rig until the spotlight circled the problem—a viciously slashed and entirely flat tire. In that instant, the eeriness of the dream vanished under the onslaught of a nightmare, and Vanessa, Jessie and I clung together in the bitter fog.

"Just what we need!" Vanessa aimed a vicious kick at the shredded tire. "I haven't changed a flat since radials arrived. Not that I'll mind having a tire iron in my hand."

At that moment, I wouldn't have minded having my

9mm in my hand. Or, at least, on my person. But I'd left my gun back at Mission Cottage, along with my good sense. Why hadn't I just stayed put and stuck with my original plan? Right then I would have welcomed a herd of the TV types—of any types!—who, presumably, still had Sam's house staked out. At least their presence back there might keep the vandal from getting into the place. Presumably slowing us down had been his aim, and the only reason I could figure for wanting that was so he could finally finish the job that had kept him lurking outside in the bushes the last few days.

"I'm scared, Mama." Jessie buried her face against me, muffling her words. "Are you?"

I pressed my lips against her silken hair. "A little bit, peanut. It's okay to be scared, you know. Being frightened can give you an edge—sharpening your hearing, warming your muscles, getting you ready to pounce."

"Pounce or be pounced." Vanessa's chuckle held no mirth. "Wanna get started on that tire?"

What to do? Both Vanessa and Jessie had asked the same question, each in her own words, but I had no answer for either of them. Changing a tire by feel, as the fog required, didn't sound promising. But surely someone in that village hall would offer assistance—once the brouhaha calmed down. Although plenty of lights had winked off in the village, every lit window that remained shone forth a promise of aid. Worst-case scenario, we could always walk home. I did have my flashlight, after all.

Far off in the distance, a foghorn groaned, reminding me of the guys who made a career out of rescue. I gave Jessie a quick squeeze. "Let's go ask the Coast Guard for help! That *is* their job."

"Fixing flat tires is part of their mission?" This time a rich humor suffused Vanessa's chuckle as I goaded my daughter and my friend into motion. "Since when?"

Towering above the docks of Hydaburg, *Le Mistral's* ghostly silhouette provided me with an unexpected measure of comfort. Just beyond, still too far to see in the fog, lay the berth of the *Kodiak.* I prodded my companions onto the planks of the pier where we marched arm in arm, our footsteps reverberating with the noise of many times our number.

As we neared the Frenchman's boat, I caught my foot on something and went down on my knees, landing hard enough to bring tears to my eyes. While Jessie and Vanessa tutted, asking over and over if I was okay, anger spurted through me, and I reached out blindly in the misty dark, feeling for the cause of my fall. My fingers found smooth metal. I snapped on my pocket flashlight long enough to recognize a squat cylinder of galvanized tin and curse the idiot who'd abandoned a can of marine varnish in my path. With one quick swipe, I heaved the varnish off the pier, enjoying a moment of satisfaction when the offending can caromed off the side of *Le Mistral.* Then I climbed to my feet, brushed off the knees of my jeans and started forward to rejoin my companions.

"Mom! Look out!"

The shrill of fear in Jessie's voice alerted me but not in time. Footsteps thunked behind me. I started to turn. A shadow emerged from the fog, huge and menacing. I lifted my arms to ward off the blow. Too late! The shadow knocked my arms aside and connected cleanly with my head, driving me back to my knees.

Pain transported me. Somewhere a child wailed and a woman growled, while my world shrank to a pin dot and then blinked off.

18

"IDIOT!" EVEN FROM A DISTANCE, RAOUL D'Onofre's furious bark penetrated the fog inside my head. "What were you thinking?"

"She attacked the ship, *mon capitaine!*" The righteous tone in the sailor's voice surprised me. Attacked the ship? "I saw her throw something that hit *Le Mistral.* I thought it was a bomb."

"A bomb!" Vanessa's angry words, spoken from somewhere close, echoed through my mind. A bomb? "You must be out of your mind."

"Mama? Wake up!" Cold and soft, Jessie's cheek pressed against mine as she spoke urgent words in my ear. "Please wake up!"

I groped for my daughter, willing myself to plunge through the aching fog that filled my head. "Hey, peanut." My hand found her small but sturdy thigh, and I opened my eyes. "I'm okay. Help me up."

"Lauren!" Stronger hands than Jessie's pressed against my shoulders. On a good night, Vanessa wouldn't have a prayer against me, but no way was this a good night. "Don't move! You may need a doctor."

A sudden stream of light blinded me. I blinked against the brilliance. *"Non!* Look at her pupils. See how they shrink?" The light vanished, and Raoul D'Onofre's face appeared before me, wreathed in a halo of after-glare. "My sincere apology, Mrs. Maxwell. I worry about sabotage, but *Le Mistral's* guards are perhaps too zealous."

"'Perhaps' nothing." Vanessa gave him an indignant snort. "Your guard is definitely a thug, and I've a mind to swear out a complaint against him!"

Jessie paid no attention to either of them and leaned into me, snuggling against my chest. "You *are* okay, aren't you, Mama? I was *soooo* scared! I don't like the fog anymore. I just want to go home."

Home! With that heartfelt sentiment, my daughter suddenly reminded me of Dorothy from *The Wizard of Oz,* and for one crazy moment, I longed for rescue by Glinda, the good witch, who could send us all back to Mission Cottage with one stroke of her magic wand. In the next moment, a good witch actually appeared.

"Mrs. Maxwell!" Nathan Chaloner fell on his knees beside me, his face a dark smudge in the enveloping fog as he looked from me to Vanessa to Raoul D'Onofre. "What's happened here?"

The Frenchman and Vanessa both spoke at once,

but I ignored their heated explanations to the Coast Guard officer, preferring to comfort myself with my kid's cuddles while I tried to concentrate long enough to judge the plausibility of D'Onofre's story. Sabotage *was* a possibility. And I *had* tossed something that could be mistaken for a bomb. Especially in the fog. But what about the Land Cruiser's tire? And what if the brooding Indian hadn't disabled the truck? Maybe D'Onofre's henchman had been following us all along! I didn't remember passing a guard stationed on the pier. If the whole thing came down to security, why hadn't we seen a guard standing watch when we approached *Le Mistral?*

The foggy air around me rang with Vanessa's outraged exclamations and D'Onofre's furious explanations, while the fog inside echoed and amplified my doubts. D'Onofre might have a plausible story, but I wasn't buying. That slashed tire combined with my aching head to send a powerful message that came in loud and clear—I'd gotten close enough to solving the riddle of Sam Houston Larrabee's death to make someone very nervous. So when Captain Nathan Chaloner offered me his assistance, I gladly accepted, requesting not only a ride home but also a guard for the night. After the briefest hesitation, he agreed and detailed the job to two young enlisted men, each armed with an M-16 rifle. In less than half an hour, Vanessa had given me a triple dose of extra strength Tylenol and then tucked me and my daughter into our bed at Mission Cottage.

Even with two armed men guarding the doors, I

slept fitfully. The Tylenol did the job on my head and my knees, reducing the sensation in both to a dull throb that finally just faded away. But nothing could ease the pain in my heart, not with one of the sources of the ache curled into a soft, warm ball beside me. What if D'Onofre's thug had missed me and conked Jessie? Bad enough that my blunder had set her up for a huge flaming fall in front of the entire world. She didn't need physical injuries to go along with the psychic wounds I expected her to sustain. Not that she'd go down without a fight. Vanessa had told me that while I lay helpless on the pier, my daughter stood over me, brandishing the flashlight like a club, while my friend grappled with my assailant. And when Raoul D'Onofre arrived on the scene, Jessie had kept him at bay, refusing to allow him near her fallen mother, until Vanessa assured herself and my daughter that no threat remained. For an instant, I wondered if a girl not schooled in competitive athletics would have had the chutzpah to fight back. For a much longer time, I wondered why any mother in her right mind would put her daughter in such a spot.

And what kind of spot would I have left both of my children in if the Frenchman's blow had been hard enough to kill me? When Max died, I learned that his life wasn't his alone. A piece of it belonged to me and to our children. With their father lost to them, our children's claim on my life became that much stronger. Jessie had been scarred by losing the father she barely remembered, and Jake had been wounded that much more deeply by losing the father he'd never forget. Knowing that, knowing what kind of heartache they'd survived, how could I lead a life that had more than once brought me close to orphaning my kids forever?

Morning finally arrived, but I'd found no easy answers. Before Jessie woke, Vanessa tempted me out of my bed with the delicious aroma of freshly ground coffee and did her damnedest to persuade me that our priority had to be finding the old woman with the mask. When I objected, insisting that getting Jess to a safer haven was my first concern, she pointed out what TV types always refer to as "grim realities." First, the press mob still surrounded Mission Cottage and, despite the presence of armed guards, showed no signs of leaving. Second, the dense layer of fog still blanketed Hydaburg, grounding all planes, which meant Jessie's only possible means of escape lay in the ferry from Hollis, a long and lonely thirty-six road miles away.

"Face it, Lauren—she's stuck here." Vanessa carefully buttered a toasted English muffin. "Unless you can convince the Coast Guard to sail her home, Jessie's going nowhere as long as this fog lasts."

The mocha java bittered my tongue, and I set my mug aside. "Maybe so, but that doesn't mean I'm going to look for that old lady. Not with Jess in tow. Not in this fog."

Vanessa folded her arms and rocked back on her heels. "So what do you want her to learn from this episode, Lauren? To hide out and wait for rescue? Is that the lesson you want to teach her? When facing danger, a woman should sit tight and hope somebody'll save her?"

Before I could reply, she spun on her heel and stalked out of the kitchen. In a second she returned with Sam Houston Larrabee's old .38 snubby in one hand. When I opened my mouth to ask what the hell she was doing, she silenced me with one stern glance. "You're not the only Annie Oakley in the crowd."

She deftly flipped open the cylinder, revolving it slowly to check for ammunition. "These days little girls who want to grow up need to learn to take responsibility for their own survival, sugar. When the bad guy's at your door, no cop or judge or brave knight's gonna save you." She snapped the cylinder closed, giving it a hard spin. "For a wise woman, there's only one solution—get a gun, learn how to use it and be prepared to shoot to kill."

In the milky light of another foggy morning, our eyes met and locked, and somehow I knew without words that we shared the same thoughts. Of Polly Klaas, a little girl who didn't fight back, didn't even scream, and never got a chance to grow up. Of Nicole Brown Simpson, a woman who expected cops and courts to protect her and paid with her life. Of Suzanna Gratia, who left her .38 behind when lunching at Luby's cafeteria and watched twenty-three people die, including her parents. I'd never favored an armed citizenry—men or women—and only after great deliberation had I been able to force myself to master the handling of the guns Max had left me. In the wild I carried a weapon in case I ran into a grizzly, but in town I'd never felt the need to arm myself against human predators. Still, there was a lot of truth to Vanessa's words. And even though I couldn't wholeheartedly endorse her solution to violence against women, I didn't want to hunker down like cornered prey or leave home the equalizer that could protect us all.

Vanessa must have sensed my train of thought. "Seems to me we've got enough firepower to keep safe while we search for that old lady." She carefully set the .38 on the kitchen table and tossed me a grin. "Could be we'll even convince those TV fellows to stay clear. Men surely do avoid a woman with a gun."

Letting her fingers do the walking, Vanessa began our search by telephone while I caught up on my E-mail. Boyce Reade reported that the response to Jessie's TV appearance continued to inundate the White House via telephone, fax, E-mail and snail mail. One enterprising enviro publicist had even rounded up a group of kindergartners, dressed them in black and white, strapped Styrofoam dorsal fins onto their backs and paraded them outside 1600 Pennsylvania Avenue and through the halls of Congress, where they chanted in unison, "Just plain mean! Just plain mean!" His most recent message summed up the current situation: *"Sympathizer inside WH reports Prez wavering, but no permits could kill renewal of marine mammal act. Congress vote tallies too close to call. Another appearance by Jessie may tilt balance in orcas' favor."*

"Damn!" Vanessa drifted back into Sam's bedroom, portable phone in hand. "Owen Stuart doesn't answer. Leona Holmes is in the classroom and can't take calls. Nadine Jackson is out in the field repairing a transmitter. And Grant Williams says the old lady sounds like half the elders in Hydaburg—the female half."

I stopped typing for a second. "Did you ask either of them if they'd heard about last night's scene at the village hall?"

Vanessa rolled her eyes and smirked. "Apparently our scene on the docks got better play at this morning's breakfast tables."

Her news allusion reminded me that Kelsey Kavanaugh owed me a bunch of favors, and I immediately called in the first marker. Identifying the old lady didn't even require her to decamp from her base inside the Sweetland Cafe. After promising to have the information "in a jiff," she merely asked the chef and then called me right back. "She lives on the outskirts of town—out your way. You want directions?"

After a quick glance through the window reassured me that the press still had us surrounded, I called in the second marker. "No, I want a ride."

An hour later, freshly scrubbed, fed and armed to the teeth, Vanessa and I escorted Jessie through the braying mob to Kelsey Kavanaugh's Ford Explorer. About three minutes later, she pulled to a stop beside a battered pickup parked outside a cedar plank house, the same house whose silvered mortuary pole that depicted Raven's discovery of the clam containing the first Haida had been explained to me by my daughter the evening she arrived in Hydaburg. As we climbed out of Kelsey's rig, the door of the small cottage swung open and the man with the brooding eyes stepped onto the stoop. While we trooped toward him, his gaze moved over us, lingering on the handguns Vanessa and I had strapped to our hips. When we stood before him, he gave us a brief nod and gestured toward the open door. "She is waiting in the kitchen."

My daughter led the way into the cheerful kitchen at the back of the house and, after pausing to admire the decorative teacups that lined the sill of the big picture window, marched up to her hostess, hand outstretched. "I'm Jessie Maxwell. Remember me?"

In her seat at one end of a cushioned bench before the window, the old woman smiled, grooving her dark face with a bounty of laugh lines. "I do indeed, child." The arm she held out boasted a red and blue tattoo of a quarter moon. "You told how Raven coaxed the first *Haada* from the clam he found on Rosespit."

As their hands met and joined, Jessie's eyes glanced from the tattoo on the elder's arm to her lips. The old woman's smile widened. "My father held a doing for my pictures, the last of its kind, but I wear no lip plug." She held out her other arm and pushed back her sleeve to reveal another red and blue design. "See the blackfish swimming here? And I have a dogfish on one leg and a grizzly bear on the other, but no labret."

While the old woman concentrated on my daughter, her companion—grandson?—seated Vanessa and me at the round kitchen table and then withdrew to the doorway, where he leaned against the frame, still lurking, still brooding. The old woman waved Jessie to a seat beside hers on the flowered chintz cushion. "How do you know the story of the *Haada?*"

"I learned it at school."

For a long moment, the old woman regarded my daughter. "Many things are learned at school, but few are remembered for long."

"I remember all of Alaska's native stories." Jessie wiggled her hips, scooting farther into the deep bench, and then lifted her dark eyes to meet the old woman's gaze. "After all, I'm a native Alaskan, too."

At that announcement, the elder's eyebrows shot up and a flash of amusement sparkled in her dark eyes. "Is that so? Then tell me another tale, Jessie Maxwell."

"Well, let's see." My daughter cocked her head and a shag of dark hair fell across her eyes. "Do you know why the eagle's feathers have the power to bring peace?"

Without waiting for a reply, she straightened, tossing the hair out of her eyes. "In the old days, heaven was very close to Earth and the people disturbed the great chief. See, every night they'd sing and make lots of noise. In the daytime, the grown-ups would sleep, but the kids would sing and make lots of noise. A shaman warned the people not to be so selfish, but they wouldn't listen."

Jessie shook her head sorrowfully. "So the great chief let all the rivers rise until only the tops of the mountains showed. Most of the people died. Eagle scattered his feathers on the water because he thought maybe the great chief would feel sorry for him and let the water go down. After eagle shed his feathers, the other birds did, too, and eventually the water did go down. To this day, eagle feathers hold the power of peace."

Jessie turned to the old woman, eyes wide with expectation, and was not disappointed. "You tell the tale well, child."

"Your turn. I know what story I want to hear." My daughter angled around until she sat facing the elder. "Tell me about the mask."

The smile fell from the old woman's face, and I held my breath. Beside me, Vanessa stiffened, but my daughter appeared perfectly at ease. After studying Jessie gravely for a few moments, the old woman turned her gaze to the man standing motionless in the doorway. He met her eyes but said nothing.

The old woman ran a hand down her arm, caressing the red and blue orca tattooed into her dark skin. "Very well. I will tell the story of the silver blackfish."

19

"YOUR PEOPLE FIRST CAME TO THE *HAADA* FOR the fur. Long time ago, every rock in the sea was a village for otter." The old woman scooped another teaspoon of sugar into her steaming cup of tea, stirring up a whirlpool. "The first of your kind came from the icy forest in the west and murdered the people of the far islands, forcing the men to kill otter and enslaving the women."

I glanced across the table at Jessie, who sat beside our hostess and calmly sipped her heavily sugared and milked tea. Like her father, my daughter is an unsentimental realist and the Russian genocide of the Aleut came as no surprise to her. Not only had she studied Alaska's brutal past in school, but she shared her home with Nina Alexeyev, whose name still bore witness to the Great Land's Russian past.

"In those days, the *Haada* lived apart on these

islands, far from the strangers from across the sea. Only later, when all the otters of the west had been killed, did they come here." She selected a homemade brownie and passed the plate to Jessie. "But the *Haada* knew of the strangers, and one night the people found one bleeding and broken on the shore. In his hand, the stranger carried a shining log."

A shining log? I wanted to interrupt, to question her on that point, but from the doorway, her young companion flashed me a warning with his stern, dark eyes. He stood apart, impassive, not eating or drinking, but more than once I'd seen his glance drift to Vanessa, whose face bore no trace of her usual good humor or more recent sorrow. Instead, a grave intensity had settled upon her features, and she leaned toward the old woman who sat across the round table.

"In those days, a great chief led the people, and seeing the broken man and the broken stuff floating upon the sea, he told the people that a great canoe had sunk just offshore." She tore a small piece from her brownie and washed it down with a sip of tea. "The shaman said the stranger's shining log held great magic, enough to protect the *Haada* from the people of the icy forest, and he wanted to gather all the shining logs from the bottom of the sea."

A wreck! My need to question our hostess almost overcame me. To restrain myself, I gripped both hands on the seat of my chair, forcing down the questions of where and when and how that rose in my throat.

"The shaman's order frightened the people because they knew that those who are lost to the sea return as blackfish. But first the dead must get their fins, and no one wanted to stop their change." She looked at the young man leaning against the door frame, meeting his eyes for a long moment before returning to her story. "The great chief was not afraid. He paddled his canoe onto the sea and went into the water."

She placed her brownie on her saucer and pushed the teacup aside. "Time and again, he sank beneath the waves, searching for the shining logs, and then climbed back into his canoe to rest and get warm." A thread of urgency entered the elder's voice. "The great chief looked for a long time and finally found the shining logs, more than he could even count! Once more he dove under the sea, but that time he never came back."

She folded her hands on the table before her. "To make peace with the dead, the shaman told the greatest carver to fashion an amulet from the shining log, and then he sank the shining blackfish with its powerful magic into the sea and declared that place forever forbidden to the *Haada.* All the shining scraps became a mask to honor the great chief, whose wife safeguarded the box to contain the evil spirit."

With the impeccable timing of a great storyteller, the old woman paused and let her gaze drift to each of us in turn, resting first on Jessie, then Vanessa and finally on me. "All of you saw that mask, and now, for the third time, I have broken my silence to tell the story of the silver blackfish."

"Did my uncle know the story?" In the doorway, the elder's companion straightened, squaring his broad shoulders. "Did he know the place?"

His uncle? At the village hall, she'd claimed the escaped evil had killed two men—one white and one Haida. If Charley Massett had been this man's uncle, what had the dead man been to her?

"From my own cursed tongue, my son heard the story of the silver blackfish." Tears welled in her eyes, and she stretched one hand across the table toward Vanessa. "And that same foolish tongue cursed your Sam as well."

Vanessa covered the old woman's hand with both of her own. "Did they search for the wreck together?"

The elder lifted her shoulders into a shrug. "I do not know. Neither told me anything."

"*Nani,* tell me where it is." He took a step toward her, and by his own word, named himself her grandson. "To find out who killed my uncle, I must go there. And you can help me."

"No!" An edge of fear sharpened her voice. "Somehow the evil once trapped by the silver amulet has been unleashed, and the wrath of the blackfish is terrible!"

The child of a different culture might have repeated his plea, but apparently the Haida produced grandsons willing to take no for an answer. However, the product of my rational approach to childrearing still had a question she wanted answered. "Why did you tell?" Jessie swung around in her chair to face the old woman. "Why, after all those years?"

For an instant, the old woman's face crumpled and tears streaked down her withered cheeks. Vanessa's hands continued to grip one of hers, but with her free hand she wiped the moisture from her face. Then she took a shuddering breath, visibly gathering herself, and erected a stoic mask. "Between that time and this, preachers came, shamans disappeared and the gods became one in Jesus Christ. With His protection, I thought I had nothing to fear."

She lifted her chin. "Now I know that, no matter who is called God, evil exists. Some blame *gageets* and some blame Satan, but I know now that evil lives in the hearts of men."

Evil. The word seemed so out of place in that cheerful kitchen. Beyond the wide picture window, fog swathed the world in a ghostly shroud, but just inside, decorative teacups lined the sill—some hand-painted with whimsical scenes, others delicately balanced on fragile footings, a few rimmed with real gold. What could a woman who collected such fancies know of evil? The very air she breathed, infused as it was with the scent of cedar, denied the existence of such dark forces. Someone once said that living in a Haida house was akin to living inside a cedar chest. How could evil hide inside a cedar chest? And yet it had. To hear the elder tell it, a simple cedar chest had managed to contain the evil of the silver blackfish for many years, even centuries. But lately death had visited Hydaburg. Twice she had spoken and twice men had died. Now the old woman had spoken again.

Did that mean another would die? The thought sent a trickle of ice down my spine.

With great effort, the old woman pushed herself erect, leaning for a moment on the sturdy table. "Of one thing you can be sure." She gazed down at Vanessa, dry-eyed now but with great weariness infecting her voice. "For all time will the *Haada* revere the memory of Sam Houston Larrabee. To us he has been a white shaman, determined to keep our stories alive."

"Let me help you, *Nani.*" Her grandson came up beside her and offered his arm. "You should rest now."

Before taking his arm, the old woman reached out and brushed her fingers across Jessie's soft cheek. "Thank you, child." Then, after nodding to me and to Vanessa, she leaned on her grandson's arm and allowed him to lead her from the kitchen.

I glanced at Vanessa, wondering whether to stay or make a run for it. She freshened her cup of tea and nudged the plate of goodies toward my daughter. After helping herself to another brownie, Jess knelt on the chintz-cushioned bench and studied the old woman's collection of teacups. I drained the last of my tepid tea and pushed the cup aside, eager to sift the old woman's tale for answers to the many questions about Sam's death but definitely uneasy about remaining in the presence of her brooding grandson. Why had he spent the last few days lurking about Mission Cottage? Nothing I'd heard from his grandmother even hinted at a solution to that little mystery.

Turned out the same problem troubled my Texas pal. When the old woman's grandson ambled back into the kitchen, Vanessa skewered him with a quick question. "How come you've been skulking around in my bushes?"

The bushwhack interrogation stopped him in mid-stride, but he recovered quickly and inclined his head in my direction. "Looking for her."

"Looking for me?" I pushed my chair back and around until I faced him. "I don't even know you."

He squared up his feet and gave me the briefest of bows. "Dan Massett."

I jumped out of the chair and stalked across the kitchen to face him straight-on. "If you were looking for me, why didn't you just come to the door? Or call me on the telephone?"

One corner of his mouth tilted into a half-smile, the first hint of good humor he'd shown. "I didn't want to meet you. I wanted to watch you."

"Watch me!" A creepy sensation ran over me, and I took a step backward. "Why did you want to watch me?"

The other corner of his mouth tilted up, and for the first time, he actually smiled. "To see if maybe you were responsible for my uncle's death." Before I could express the outrage I felt, he shot a quick glance at Jessie. "Why don't we discuss this outside?"

Leaving Vanessa to occupy my daughter, I followed him onto the front stoop, hoping the fog would hide us from any news snoops who happened by, and leaned against the rough cedar planks. "You're not the first person to suspect me of murder, you know. Last time I faced down the FBI." For tone of voice, I aimed at bravado. "So what tipped you off? My gun?"

He raised his eyebrows. "Your skin. Sneak attack is not the way of my people."

That insight shut me up and he took advantage of my silence to continue. "I was out of town when it happened. When I got back, my grandmother told me that Charley's death had something to do with Sam's. But that's all she told me—until today. I took a hard look at all of you—Owen Stuart, Leona Holmes, Raoul D'Onofre, Nadine Jackson, Grant Williams and you. Anybody who knew Sam Larrabee was suspect." He lifted his shoulders into a shrug. "By now, I've crossed most of the names off my list."

My turn to raise my eyebrows. "Who's left?"

He gave me a three-count before answering. "Stuart and D'Onofre."

"Why them?"

Another shrug. "They knew Sam and they know boats."

His reasoning sounded too simple, too pat, and I bristled. "That makes them killers? For what? A sunken treasure? That sounds so ludicrous." I spread my arms wide. "Owen Stuart doesn't care about anything but his precious whales. And Raoul D'Onofre? He's got an aquarium ready to pay him millions! What would either of them want with some old silver amulet?"

"More millions?" He tilted his head to study me. "You don't get it, do you? This isn't about an amulet. This is about 'shining logs.' Lots and lots of 'shining logs.'"

I rested fisted hands on my hips. "Maybe you'd better explain."

"Those early Russians traded with China, and the Chinese accepted only two kinds of goods from barbarians—furs or specie." He folded his arms and leaned back against the door. "Finding enough fur could be chancy, so a wise merchant captain carried plenty of specie. That way, if he didn't find fur, he could still trade for silk and tea."

I let out a sigh. "What does this specie have to do with anything?"

"Specie usually means coins, but I'm betting those 'shining logs' are bars about yea big." He spread his hands about two feet apart. "Solid silver bars—lots and lots of 'em." He refolded his arms. "Only one way to find out. We'll have to locate that wreck."

We? I gave him a quick once-over then, noting the wide shoulders that filled his gray sweatshirt, the sturdy legs encased in dungarees, the dark eyes clear and, for once, unguarded. Although I hadn't come to the Massett house in search of a partner, it looked like I'd found one. "Think you can convince your grandmother to tell us the location?"

He shook his head. "Not a chance. But I've got a pretty good idea where to look."

I flung my arms wide. "Even so, I'll need someone to help me! I can't dive alone."

His grin widened into a smile as he pushed up the sleeve of his sweatshirt to reveal a large blue tattoo of an eagle rampant on anchor and trident and wreathed with words: United States Navy SEAL. "I'd be happy to come along."

20

Pink ribbons of dawn streamed across the sky the next morning when Dan Massett's battered Ford pickup rattled into the drive at Mission Cottage. Although the press pack had diminished considerably, a few obstinate fellows surged forward, peppering our new partner with sullen questions. He and Vanessa held them off while I tossed Jessie's gear bag atop a collection of diving equipment in the bed of the truck and then bundled my sleepy daughter into the cab. Her drowsiness had silenced the objections to our plan that she'd voiced the night before. Any kid could benefit from a day spent with a grandmother, especially one who baked such great brownies. And searching for the Russian wreck would be tedious enough without a restless soon-to-be nine-year-old in tow.

At his grandmother's house, Massett carried Jessie's bag inside while I shepherded my kid into the spare bedroom and tucked her in under a real Chilkat blanket. His grandmother reserved her smiles and her words for Jess, but he bent down to brush a quick kiss across her withered cheek. "We'll be fine, *Nani.* I promise you." Then we were off to the waterfront where he parked the pickup well away from the fee-for berths at the town docks and near a flotilla of moored water craft that included the striking cedar dugout I'd noticed a few days before. In the early morning twilight, the carved and painted eagle on the prow seemed to swoop across the water.

I hoisted a pair of air tanks and a mesh bag filled with diving gear from the bed of the truck. "Which one is yours?"

He pointed to the dugout riding so proudly on the gentle swell. "That one."

Vanessa looked from the dugout to Massett. "She's beautiful. Did you carve her?"

"You bet." He grabbed another pair of air tanks. "For racing, not for diving. That's where I was when Charley died. At a competition in BC." He gestured toward a small, rusty trawler anchored beside his Haida canoe. "We'll use a friend's boat today."

He started for the path to the beach, and I followed, with Vanessa bringing up the rear. "Another eagle, but not the one you've got on your arm."

He tossed me a grin over his shoulder. "This one's my birthright. Massetts are an eagle clan."

During the night, a short, furious storm finally had swept the fog from Prince of Wales Island, leaving the air clear and the sea smooth. I stowed the last of the gear belowdecks and joined Vanessa and Dan Massett on the bridge as he piloted the borrowed boat out of Hydaburg harbor. Lights showed on the larger ships at the town pier, but as far as I could tell, nothing else moved on the water. He laid in a course for the Tlevak Strait side of Sukkwan Island, explaining that the present town had been founded only eighty years earlier by the last residents of three small Haida villages. "My people—*Nani's* people—came from Sukkwan, and that's where we'll find the wreck."

An hour later, he eased back on the throttle and let the trawler idle on the water before a narrow, rocky cove. At one end, a twisted Sitka spruce clung to an offshore rock with roots like gnarled tentacles, and in the center, a scatter of boulders dotted the stony shore. "This is it. In all the days we spent out here, this is the one cove I can't ever remember entering. When I asked my uncle about it, he just shrugged and said, 'Nothing good will come from there.' "

He leaned on the wheel. "The sea can get a little squirrely around here. You've got the Alaska Current running counterclockwise up toward the Aleutians, but the prevailing wind's out of the northwest. Depending on weather conditions when the Russian sank, the debris could be just about anywhere."

Vanessa stood beside him, one arm braced on the bulkhead. "Pardon my inexperience, but how do you do this? Just dive in and start finning?"

He reached down and unlatched the door of a cupboard in the bulkhead next to the wheel, swinging it open to reveal an array of metered gauges, and then tapped one piece of equipment. "I set up this magnetometer last night. We'll tow it behind the boat in a grid pattern looking for any deviations in the earth's magnetic field caused by iron on the bottom. The charts show the deepest spot's only thirty-five feet—well within our range."

Dan Massett took charge of the search, assigning himself the task of steering the trawler in squares across an imaginary grid while Vanessa monitored the magnetometer in the wheelhouse for signs of iron and I took up position on deck, standing ready to slip a marker buoy over the side whenever we got a solid hit. Before we started, he hauled twenty buoys onto the deck, every one of them attached by forty feet of line to a stubby plug of cement anchor but each sporting a different paint job. I hefted a blue buoy with a trio of white crosses. "Looks like you expect to find lots of litter down there. Where'd you get all of these?"

"The buddy who owns this boat does some crabbing." He scanned the narrow cove. "I expect to find more than enough to leave us mighty confused. At least to start."

No joke! In the 45,000 years since early humans first took to the salt, the planet's coastal waters have accumulated plenty of junk. With placid seas and calm winds, Massett needed only an hour to trace the magnetometer over the entire cove, and in that time, I placed fourteen buoys to mark hits while Vanessa charted each find and recorded the actual magnetic reading. As we searched, the shadows cast upon the water by the rising sun retreated, bringing full light. Each time Vanessa recorded a magnetic anomaly, she poked her head out of the wheelhouse to tell me to drop a buoy over the stern. In between hits, I hunkered down on deck while the pair on the bridge chattered like old pals. When we'd finished the search pattern, Massett let the boat drift with the current and broke out the snacks, pouring steaming mugs of hot chocolate for each of us and insisting I eat a couple of high-energy power bars. "You'll need 'em down there."

He leaned against the bulkhead to study Vanessa's record of the magnetometer readings and then circled five spots she'd charted which indicated significant amounts of iron. "Cannons or anchor, anchor chain or cannon balls—that's my guess."

She peered at the papers he held. "I thought cannons were brass."

He gave her a crooked smile. "Russians have never been known for elegance in weaponry or shipbuilding. From what I've been taught, they've always preferred to keep things simple and cheap. After all, they didn't need brass cannons to whip Napoleon."

Vanessa stayed topside to man the bridge while Massett and I changed into diving gear. He'd brought an assortment of neoprene, and after I tried on various combinations, we settled on a Farmer John body suit worn under the long-sleeved top from a full wet suit, both three-eighths of an inch thick. Back on deck, I sorted through the gear bags for a hood and a mask plus booties, gloves and fins, while he checked the gauges on the air tanks. Despite the cool morning air, sweat popped out on my forehead as I snugged the hood into the top of my wet suit. "Those seventy-twos only hold about forty-five minutes of air." I tightened the wrist strap on one glove. "Will ninety minutes be enough time?"

He rocked back on his haunches and gave me a searching look. "Water in the strait's about fifty-six degrees this time of year. At that temperature, ninety minutes could seem like forever."

I settled the mask on top of my hood and then met his appraisal head-on. "At my most courageous, I still prefer caution to carelessness. Today I'll defer to your greater experience. You call the shots."

Dan Massett's first shot called for beginning the search by investigating a cluster of three buoys near the center of the cove. After motoring close to the one farthest from shore, he dropped the anchor and gave Vanessa strict instructions on handling the wheel and the throttle should the need arise. Then he positioned a boarding ladder on the side of the boat, gripped the mouthpiece of his regulator between his teeth and led me into the sea's cold embrace.

For a moment, I lingered on the surface, riding out that first shock when the icy water penetrates the suit, but then I executed a quick jackknife, letting the force of my rising legs propel me after Dan Massett, who'd followed the buoy's anchor line toward the bottom. Underwater, an eerie other world exists, a cool murky place of effortless motion and soft landings. A human traveling in that weightless world comes close to flying, swooping and soaring in a wet and euphoric wild blue yonder. But then other sensations intrude. The absolute pressure weighs against the eardrum, producing ear squeeze, and against the mask, producing mask squeeze, painful reminders that the ocean world is an alien and dangerous habitat. The density of the water refracts the light, making objects appear closer and larger than they really are, a disorientating distortion that slows both action and reaction. And a thick mist of diatoms, the one-celled creatures at the bottom of the sea's food chain, reduces visibility to feet, enclosing the air-breathing alien in a small clearing surrounded by endless gloom.

From below me rose a lazy string of bubbles that provided an easy path to my companion. He waited just above the buoy's anchor, which had landed atop a small tumble of rocks. He hung upright and peered across the jumbled rocks that dotted smooth sands on the ocean's floor. As I slid into view, he crooked a finger and indicated I should position myself beside him. When I had, he unsnapped a coiled rope from his weight belt, clipped the carabiner to mine, spooled out the line to show me the evenly spaced knots and then signaled his intention of searching in concentric rings at five-foot intervals with me standing fast at the bull's-eye. I nodded, circling my thumb and index finger to flash the hand signal for okay.

Midway through the first circle, he stopped, reappearing within seconds with a crushed ammunition can in his hand, the watertight kind used by rafters to keep their gear dry. He tipped it over, emptying muck inside that sifted slowly back toward the bottom. From the looks of the can's smooth sides, that particular piece of litter hadn't been in the water all that long. With another carabiner from his weight belt, he snapped the crushed ammo can to the buoy line and then consulted the compass he'd strapped to one wrist as I recoiled the knotted search rope.

After Massett oriented himself, he led the way toward the second buoy, his flippers kicking up small clouds of silt as he finned. I swam beside and a little behind him, gliding close to the bottom until a protrusion of rocks forced me to sweep up and over, startling a school of tiny fish which darted away, quicksilver streaks through the twilight. Up ahead, a red-and-white buoy line bisected the water, the red faded to gray at this depth.

This anchor had fallen onto clear silt. After I took up position beside it, Massett moved away, unstringing the knotted rope. I held my place, twirling slowly as the line moved, hearing only the sound of my own breathing and seeing nothing after Massett disappeared into the gloom. He had almost completed two circuits before stopping again. This time the magnetic anomaly turned out to be the heavily encrusted blade of a handleless shovel, the wide and deep kind firemen once used to scoop coal into steamship boilers.

After another compass reading, Massett angled toward shore to find the third buoy. Brown ruffle-edged blades of sugar wrack rose from the rocky bottom, swaying gently in the current, and green clumps of sea lettuce sprouted here and there. Massett swam straight through the bed of kelp, using both hands to part the plants. The rubbery blades swung back into place, forcing me also to push them aside. When one snagged around my arm, I experienced a tiny spurt of panic and forced myself to untangle the kelp, even though I knew one firm jerk of my arm would free me. The adrenaline had barely subsided when I emerged from the forest of kelp to find Dan Massett spinning circles around a buoy line like an underwater trapeze artist, a wide grin and dancing eyes clearly visible through the glass of his mask. Beneath him, the stubby plug of concrete that anchored the buoy had landed squarely atop a scabrously encrusted object that bore the unmistakable silhouette of an old-time ship's cannon.

The wreck! My heart clonged again, partly from joy and partly from terror, and to hide my confusion, I plastered a grin on my face and somersaulted toward my partner. Long, long ago, teredo worms had consumed all the wood of the Russian ship while other sea creatures had stripped flesh from the human wreckage and salt had slowly dissolved bone. But even so, even with only the iron of the Russian ship remaining, the rusting cannon marked the site of a tragedy, a place where men from half a world away had met their deaths, far from home and crying for their mothers or their wives as the ocean took them, lashed by storm and surge and surf as they struggled for one last breath of blessed air. A great chief had also died here, a man with the courage to do the shaman's bidding but not the stamina to long withstand the relentless power of the sea. And perhaps the site had claimed another victim as well.

This time Dan Massett clipped the search line to the cannon and together we swam in concentric circles around the wreckage. At five feet, he spotted a blackened lump that might contain the hinge of a door. At ten feet, I pointed to a mound that turned out to be an anchor chain. A little further, the smooth bottom gave way to puckered ground, a series of washed-out dimples in the silt. At fifteen feet, another set of random depressions dimpled the ocean floor.

Dan Massett hovered above the disturbed ground and pointed down before pantomiming digging. Someone had been here and not that long ago. But the evidence of digging proved nothing by itself. Perhaps those random patterns represented random searches which uncovered nothing. Or perhaps those random patterns marked the spots where bars of silver, wrenched from the guts of a dying ship, had been randomly strewn across the ocean bottom. In another few days, even that scant evidence would vanish, the bottom swept smooth again by the ceaseless tides.

At thirty feet and at forty feet, more depressions appeared, and at the last set, my partner paused again. He checked his watch and then pointed to the surface. For the first time since the adrenaline hit while I swam through the kelp bed, I noticed the chill of the water and my energy flagged. Someone had been here—we knew that much—but the who and when and why remained unanswered.

The thought drained me even more, and I was

about to start for the surface when another silt-dusted silhouette caught my eye. With one hard kick, I swam toward the object, arms outstretched before me to brush the silt away from the still-gleaming blade of a sturdy diving knife. Sam's knife?

My gloved fingers closed around the hilt. Vanessa would know. After all, the diving knife had been her graduation gift to him.

21

BEFORE SIDESTEPPING UP THE BOARDING LADDER, I carefully zipped the diving knife into the sleeve of my wet suit. Vanessa darted out of the wheelhouse, hand outstretched to assist me and eyes bright with expectation. "Any luck?"

"Yes and no." Dan Massett heaved himself out of the water. "We found the wreck, but the treasure's gone. Somebody beat us to it."

After supporting me until I settled myself against the gunwale, she offered her hand to him as he stepped from the ladder onto the boat. "Any idea who could have taken it?"

I peeled off my gloves and mask, letting them slip to the deck, and then unzipped the sleeve of my wet suit, bringing out the diving knife and displaying it across my palm. "Does this look familiar, Vanessa?"

Covering her mouth with one hand, she nodded

slowly and carefully lifted the knife from my palm. For a long moment, she turned it this way and that, appraising the molded rubber handle and sharp serrated blade. While she studied the knife, I studied her, noting that neither her hand nor her lips trembled and her eyes remained dry. She *was* getting better. Finally, her gaze lifted. "It's Sam's. I gave it to him the day he graduated from UT."

I spread my arms but remained seated. "I'd give you a hug, but I'd leave you sopping."

She gave me a slow smile and leaned down to rest her cheek against the dripping neoprene hood that covered my head. "That's all right, sugar. You've been a tower of strength for too long."

I glanced at Dan Massett, who balanced on one bare foot in the middle of the deck while removing the fin and bootie from the other. "That knife clears up a couple of questions. Like where Sam actually died. And why. But what about your uncle? How was he involved?"

"Don't know." He dropped his other fin and bootie to the deck, then came up beside me to lift the paired seventy-twos from my back. "But I've got some questions of my own. If the silver on that wreck was the motive for murder, then why are both Raoul D'Onofre and Owen Stuart still in Hydaburg?"

He leaned the backpack of air tanks against the wheelhouse, next to his own. "I'd figured one of them for the killer, but now I'm not so sure. Logically, the killer should take the treasure and run. Why stick around? The only reason I can think of is that there's something still down there."

Vanessa inserted Sam's knife into the center of a coil of rope and then knelt to help me off with my booties and fins. "Who ever said killers acted logically? And what could be down there? You said yourself that the silver's gone."

Nodding, he shrugged out of his wet suit top. "Those bars would have been hard to miss. But maybe the killer's after something smaller and more difficult to find."

"The orca amulet!" Despite the welcome warmth of the sun, I shivered. "But how valuable could that really be? Even a few silver bars would be worth a fortune. Why risk a real treasure for an ornament that might be damaged beyond repair? Saltwater is hell on silver. Anything immersed for long would be extensively sulfided."

Dan Massett's dark eyes clouded as he stared across the sea. "Remember what *Nani* said at the village hall? 'The evil spirit was contained.' And later in her kitchen? 'The shining blackfish with its terrible power.'" His eyes cleared and his glance moved first to Vanessa and then to me. "Perhaps that's what the killer wants—that terrible power."

"Hold it right there." I threw up a hand signaling him to stop. "I've got great respect for your grandmother and for your people, Dan, but that's just a little too witch doctory for me. Both of the men you suspect are scientists, for God's sake, and eminently rational men! I can't see either one of them buying into an evil amulet."

Vanessa rocked back on her heels and balanced before me. "First he wants his killers to act logically; now you want your scientists to behave rationally." She tapped her chest with one index finger. "I'm here to tell you that maybe they do and maybe they don't. Both of you make the assumption that this killer is sane." She waggled her finger. " 'Tain't necessarily so."

Vanessa's insight put an end to our speculation. Massett led her back to the bridge, setting a course and putting the boat in motion under her control before disappearing below to change into dry clothing. I remained on deck to collect the assortment of diving gear and stow everything in mesh bags designed to prevent the onset of mildew before we reached shore. When our partner reappeared in the wheelhouse, I took my turn below.

A narrow berth filled most of the space but the thick terry cloth towel invited me to linger. Vigorously rubbing my chilled skin, I gazed through the small porthole and considered Vanessa's words. She doubted the killer's sanity, expecting neither logic nor reason. How did that doubt square with what I knew of Massett's suspects? Irresponsible—that's what I'd called Raoul D'Onofre after he recklessly and needlessly risked a sailor's life during a capture drill.

I lifted the terry cloth to my head to dry my hair, toweling carefully so I wouldn't press too hard on the tender spot. And what about the thug he sent to club me down? Perhaps the Frenchman's security arrangements spoke less of precaution and more of paranoia.

After reaching for the soft polypropylene that provided the layer closest to my skin, I pulled the shirt over my head and stood up to tuck it into my jeans. And what about Owen Stuart? Sure, the cetacean biologist talked to himself, but so what? These days the range of normal behaviors had broadened to include eccentricities that earlier eras had deemed insanity. But did normal now include the notion that orcas represented the most evolved species on earth, one that ruled its world with more intelligence than man showed in ruling his?

I finished buttoning my denim shirt and grabbed my polar fleece pullover, knotting the sleeves around my shoulders. My daughter had suggested that Owen liked orcas more than he liked people. And maybe he did. But did that make him insane?

Back in the wheelhouse, I found my companions engrossed by the chatter emanating from the boat's radio. Vanessa jerked a thumb at the squawk box. "Better listen up, sugar. Sounds like big doings back in Hydaburg."

For a moment, the static and voices subsided, so I tossed in a question. "What's going on?"

Dan Massett held his position at the wheel but allowed his gaze to drift in my direction. A new burst of babble from the radio forced him to raise his voice. "From the sounds of the blab, the orca hunt is on out in the Sukkwan Strait."

His words hit with the force of a typhoon, buckling

my knees. The radio chatter blurred into an aggravating buzz, and I leaned against the bulkhead for support. "I've got to get out there. You've got to take me."

"I can't." He tapped one of the gauges on the console. "I'm too low on fuel. And my buddy's got a salmon charter scheduled for later today."

A horrifying tide of helplessness swept over me. The decisive moment had finally arrived, and I'd missed it. The battle had begun, and I'd gone AWOL. Now my boss *would* have my head—probably my job, too—and who could blame him?

Vanessa slipped an arm around me and gave me a firm hug. "Don't you fret, Lauren. Daniel's got this boat moving at maximum speed and he's heading straight for the town dock. You'll find yourself a charter and be out there in no time."

I snagged my lower lip between my teeth, tasting salt, and resisted the urge to cry as the radio crackled with messages, some cryptic gibberish and others easily understood, with seafarers spouting ranges in yards and bearings in degrees while newsmen queried about *Le Mistral*'s location and D'Onofre's quarry. Massett's borrowed boat plowed through a placid sea that flowed between dazzling green mountains arrayed under a brilliant blue sky, but in the doorway of the wheelhouse, I remained blind to the beauty that surrounded me. My mind blanked except for one word that repeated endlessly: faster, *faster, FASTER!*

As Dan Massett changed course at the gong buoy marking the channel to Hydaburg, I gazed to the south where the ecoarmada steamed away without me. Faster, *faster, FASTER!*

At last, the port of Hydaburg came into view, but the docks appeared virtually deserted. A few rusting tubs rode at anchor beside Dan Massett's Haida dugout. Along the pier, several other boats remained, each with an engine in some state of disassembly. After tossing a hurried thanks over my shoulder to my companions, I trotted down the wharf, heading for the troller I'd chartered the week before, but in my absence, the Haida skipper had probably gotten a better offer and his berth proved to be as empty as all the others. All except the one containing Owen Stuart's Zodiac raft. And the man himself stood beside the wheel.

"I didn't expect to find you in port." I stopped next to his berth, awkward in his presence because of my earlier doubts about his sanity. And worse. "Is it true that D'Onofre's permits came through?"

"So I am told." He turned toward me, holding up a hand to shield his eyes from the sun. "No need for me to rush off yet. My hydrophones are silent."

I glanced at the silent receiver mounted behind the wheel of the Zodiac. "Where are the orca pods?"

He shrugged, dropping his hand and his face. "I do not know. Even after all these years, they still keep secrets from me." He brushed his fingers across the hydrophone receiver. "But when the orcas move into harm's way, I will be the first to know."

I danced from foot to foot, unable to disguise my impatience. "When are you going out there?"

Another shrug. "Soon."

"Take me with you!" I stepped toward him, resting a foot on the tube of his raft. "I've got to get out there!"

He frowned deeply and shook his head. "That would not be wise. I have made a commitment to stop this barbarity, and if necessary, I will take direct action against the whalers."

I leaned toward him. "What do you mean?"

He looked at me then, blue eyes as icy as an Arctic sea. "I will do anything—anything, everything, whatever it takes—to prevent the capture of any orca."

The merciless certainty of Owen Stuart's words gave me pause. Was he ruthless enough to slash Sam's air hose? Was he vicious enough to obliterate Charley Massett? To what end? His only interest—his obsession—was the orcas, and in no way did either Sam Houston Larrabee or Charley Massett figure in the fate of those whales. Which meant that Owen Stuart had no motive to murder either man. I pushed aside the last niggling doubt. And even if I was wrong, what harm could come to me if I went with him? With all the TV cameras on hand, the whole world literally was watching. Not to mention the Coast Guard and, for all I knew, the FBI, if Colleen Malloy had managed to get back in time for the big show.

I dropped to my knees, resting atop the tubes of the cetacean biologist's raft. "Owen, please, you have to take me with you. This whole thing is my fault. If it weren't for my stupid miscalculation, the President wouldn't have considered issuing permits to capture orcas. So far, nothing I've done has changed his decision. If direct action is our only chance to stop this, then so be it." I clasped my hands together, completing the picture of the penitent. "I'll do whatever it takes—anything and everything—to protect the orcas."

As I spoke, his eyes had clouded but now they cleared, and a smile of real enthusiasm spread across his lips. "Very well, my dear."

He offered his hand to help me onto the Zodiac, and his fingers closed around mine with a firm, almost painful grip. "As you have seen for yourself, having you aboard on this final voyage is most fitting."

22

For a second, as his hand crushed mine and he spoke of final voyages, panic seized me. I tottered on the raft tube, leaning back toward the dock as I considered my chances for escape and measured the distance from my foot to his crotch. But then his grip loosened and his smile softened. "I finally have enough saved to replace this garbage scow. My new boat will be on tomorrow's Hollis ferry."

What a difference a few words made! I hopped into the raft and he released my hand, waving me toward the bow. "Find a life jacket and we will be off." He tapped the silent hydrophone receiver again. "Although, as I say, there is no need to rush."

Finding the fleet wasn't hard. As soon as Stuart's Zodiac cleared the harbor, we came upon the tail of the mob, which had swung around and steamed north over the water I'd just crossed with Dan Massett and

Vanessa. Such aimless wandering wasn't the only crazy aspect of that weird armada. The scene in the Sukkwan Strait resembled a regatta scripted by the Mad Hatter. The propellers of dozens of boats had churned the water into a frenzied chop that bucked Stuart's Zodiac, which jerked this way and that, rearing up and then slapping back against the water as waves broke from every direction. I clung to the rescue rope that looped around the raft like a party sash and craned forward to get my bearings. I recognized *Rainbow Warrior* and the Sea Shepherd Conservation Society's motor vessel amid the smaller fishing and pleasure craft all jockeying for position. Sea spray created a fine mist that hung low over the surface, reducing visibility and leaving the most distant ships indistinct blurs on the horizon. Far ahead, I thought I detected the bold red slash that marked USCG *Kodiak* and spared a thought for Captain Nathan Chaloner, who surely considered this seaborne pandemonium a disaster waiting to happen. After searching in vain for *Le Mistral's* brilliant white and blue, I turned back toward the cetacean biologist, cupping a hand so my words wouldn't be snatched away by the breeze. "I don't see D'Onofre's ship. Do you?"

Squinting against sun and mist, he scanned the sea ahead, tracing a 180-degree arc that encompassed the entire mad fleet, and then shook his head. "At this rate, we never will." He gave the wheel a sharp tug, sending the raft into a tight turn toward the north. "I will skirt this mob. Find the glasses in the compartment under your seat, train them on the pack and sing out when you spot *Le Mistral.*"

At full throttle, even the soft Alaskan air stung my cheeks and I welcomed the protection of Owen Stuart's binoculars. I stretched out in the bow, legs anchored on the deck and elbows propped against the seat cushion to support the glasses glued to my eyes. As the raft hugged the shore, the ride smoothed out, leaving me less likely to bonk myself in the forehead with every wave. The westering sun sent shadows fingering across the water, purple splotches that created an artificial dusk which strained my vision. The glare off the water left bright motes dancing across my eyes even in those shadowed patches of twilight. So blinded was I that *Le Mistral* had been in my sights for some time before I recognized her. "There she is!" I raised my head from the binoculars and flung out an arm. "Heading this way! Do you see her?"

For an answer, Stuart steered the Zodiac toward the Frenchman's whaler, coming in at an angle, and I settled back down with the binoculars to study his progress. To my immense gratification, Raoul D'Onofre's Zodiac and runabouts remained on deck, safely tied down and covered with fitted canvas. But a new array of ominous-looking gear had appeared on *Le Mistral,* including a trio of objects—one at the stern, one amidships and one at the bow—that looked suspiciously like guns, resembling as they did the naval artillery I remembered from the gung-ho war movies of my childhood. Before them lay an enormous net in one long neat pile. I rolled onto one elbow and shouted back to Owen Stuart, "When did he trick out those guns?"

The cetacean biologist lifted his gaze to the deck of the whaler and studied D'Onofre's new cannons, visible above the rail even at this distance.

I pointed to the canvas-covered boats on the ship's deck. "He's still got his gear under wraps. Do you think maybe he's heading home?"

His mouth settled into a stern line, and he just shrugged.

I rolled back onto both elbows, raised the binoculars and kept the whaler under surveillance as *Le Mistral* emerged from the mist. She held course for the harbor and came on steadily. Apparently several of the other boats had answered my question affirmatively because they too turned off, circling back toward the bedlam in the strait. News types, most likely, and eager for film footage of the mad regatta. Steady on came the whaler and even more boats wheeled away, heading back toward the pack.

I'd let my gaze drift while I considered declaring the outing a false alarm, but a new object rose into view, a shining black triangle that emerged from the water about one hundred feet off the Frenchman's bow.

The appearance of that dorsal fin struck terror in my heart. D'Onofre had an orca in his sights!

"Oh, shit!" I scrambled to my feet, yanking the strap of the binoculars from my neck. "He's closing on an orca!" I shoved the glasses at Stuart. "See for yourself!"

I grabbed the wheel as he grabbed the binoculars,

holding course and speed steady while he glassed first the sea—"Q 34! What the bloody hell is he doing here?"—and then the ship—"Those aren't weapons! Those guns will fire the net!"

He lowered the binoculars and fiddled for a moment with his hydrophone receiver, tracing a finger over a fresh scratch in the black metal. "Bastard! His bully boys scratched the case when they disabled the receiver."

He faced me then, a terrible emptiness leaving his eyes bleak. "Those runabouts were all for show, to mislead the people and the press. He never intended to herd the orcas into a cove. He'll fire a net over them and create an instant cage!"

I studied the deck of *Le Mistral,* where three sailors had taken up positions behind the guns while several others checked the piled net. "I don't understand."

"He'll shoot that net from the deck of his whaler." Stuart raised a hand, fingers spread, and sketched the capture scenario against the blue sky. "The outer edge will be weighted to carry it rapidly to the bottom, but flotation devices inside will buoy the center, to keep the orca from drowning."

"Like a net parachute!" Now I could visualize D'Onofre's instant cage. "Except that it won't collapse. The floats will keep the center on the surface and the weights will pin the edges to the bottom."

The grim line of Owen Stuart's mouth firmed as he took the wheel back. After checking the throttle to make sure I'd maintained maximum speed, he corrected our heading, steering to intersect not with *Le*

Mistral but with the whale instead. "All right, then. If he wants Q 34, he will have to take us as well."

As we neared the Frenchman's whaler, the deck towered high above our puny raft like an unscalable cliff of riveted steel. The sailors fussing with the nets had disappeared, but the other trio remained at their stations by the net guns. After three blows, Q34 had sounded again, and Owen Stuart kept track of his dive, counting off the time in fifteen-second intervals as we closed the distance with *Le Mistral.* On the deck above, the sailor manning the center gun suddenly took a step forward and stood just behind the net, waving both arms high above his head and shouting words that the wind instantly carried away.

"One hundred and five seconds." Stuart eased off the throttle, slowing the Zodiac as he steered into a tight circle a mere dozen yards off the Frenchman's starboard bow. "Get ready."

Ready for what? A spurt of adrenaline sent my heartbeat into overdrive, preparing me for fight or flight, even though I could do neither. Just ahead, the point of *Le Mistral's* bow plowed green water, tossing back a foaming white curl. Could I fight the man-made leviathan that bore down on us? At the wheel of the Zodiac, Owen Stuart remained rock steady, determined to win his insane game of chicken. Could I flee without a boat? Swim for it, perhaps?

KWHOOF! With one enormous, fish-oily blow, the orca reappeared a half-dozen yards beyond Stuart's

Zodiac, his six-foot dorsal fin clearly marking his position.

Cr-crack! The guns aboard *Le Mistral* fired, and the net soared away from the deck, snaking through the air. Owen Stuart bellowed, his red face torqued with rage, and shook a fist above his head. I slid to the floor of the Zodiac, figuring the tubes would protect me from the weight of the net. The rope canopy billowed toward us, imprinting black grids upon blue sky as it streamed above the sea. Streamed and then stopped with a jerk, like a dog reaching the end of its tether.

I glanced back at *Le Mistral,* where the sailor in charge of the center gun stood with arms folded, his unfired gun still anchoring a portion of the net. Then I lifted my gaze to the net above me, the leading edge carrying evenly spaced weights that even now plummeted toward the sea.

Toward the Zodiac!

Straight at Owen Stuart!

I screamed a warning as the net hissed down. "Look out!"

At my shout, he lunged toward me, landing in my lap as the net sliced the air around us, falling just short of the raft. Only one weight hit the Zodiac, but that was enough.

POP!

As the heavy ring of steel connected with the stern, a tube burst like a balloon, giving one explosive gasp of air before settling into a steady wheeze of deflation. Clear green seawater surged into the raft.

The cetacean biologist scrambled to his feet and

lurched across the tilting deck for the console in the middle of the Zodiac. I struggled to stand as Stuart yanked aside the cargo net, pawing aside extra life jackets and ammo cans as he dug for the orange neoprene survival suits. He pulled one free and held it out to me. "Put this on quickly."

The bow wash of the whaler hit the Zodiac, rocking the little raft as the stern settled into the water. I crouched in the bow, steadying myself against the slow rise of the deck so I could slip my legs into the survival suit. The engines of *Le Mistral* screamed as the ship's propellers spun into reverse, churning the sea at the stern into white water. After shucking my life jacket, I ducked inside the suit, hands and fingers searching for the sleeves.

In the middle of the raft, as the water rose to his knees, Owen Stuart struggled into his survival suit. After yanking the neoprene to his hips, he fumbled with the fasteners of his life jacket but the bottom clasp wouldn't open. After successive failures, he tried a new tack, loosening the lowest belt that snugged the life jacket against his hips. Then with a grunt, he raised the still fastened jacket from his waist, wiggling until his shoulders came through. But the fastener snagged the thick sweater he wore under his life jacket, yanking that up as well, leaving his head swathed in a ludicrous turban that blinded him to the sparkle of light that flashed from the pendant hanging from a chain around his neck. Gleaming silver against the red mat of hair on Stuart's chest lay a blackfish carved in the Haida style.

The orca amulet!

The sight froze my heart and robbed me of breath. Owen Stuart! The killer! If he had the amulet, he had to be the one who killed Sam.

With another grunt, the cetacean biologist freed himself from the sweater and life jacket knotted above his head. I forced my eyes away, busying myself with the heavy zipper that bisected my survival suit from hip to neck. Had the roar of *Le Mistral*'s engines drowned my gasp at the sight of unmistakable proof of Owen Stuart's guilt? Would he interpret my widened eyes as a symptom of terror at the idea of giving myself over to the sea? After pulling the zipper tightly into place, I risked another glance at Owen Stuart.

"Catch!" He tossed me a sheathed fishing knife, and his face twisted with his snarl. "Use that to fix his bloody net." His eyes glittered. "Cut the bloody thing to pieces."

I studied the knife in my hand. Was this the one that sent Sam Houston Larrabee to his death? Then, as a wave broke over the bow of the sinking Zodiac raft, I followed Owen Stuart into the sea.

23

WITH ONE FINAL BURP OF AIR, THE RAFT SLIPPED beneath the green seawater, leaving me adrift with a killer. The buoyancy of the survival suit made maneuvering difficult, forcing me onto my back to ride high on the water like a bobber. Despite the insulation of the neoprene, the chill of the water numbed my legs and the breeze stung my exposed skin. Owen Stuart managed to scull to the whaler's net. "Come on!" He clambered atop one of the net's floats, balancing precariously with wide-spread arms. In one hand, he held a knife. "Help me cut the bloody net!"

The net spilled from amidships of *Le Mistral* and spread across the surface, kept afloat by a series of large blue buoys. Under the water, a curtain of weighted net hung toward the bottom. "Where's the orca?" I paddled myself in a tight circle to scan the surface for 360 degrees, finding the going rough with one hand mostly given over to gripping a knife and the chop of the sea slapping water in my face. "Did they get him?"

In answer, Stuart pointed to the north. A cloud of vapor erupted from Q34's shining black back before his dorsal fin vanished from our world again. "Come on then!" The biologist leaned back to his work, hacking away at Raoul D'Onofre's net. "Fix this bleeding net."

High above, *Le Mistral*'s horn sounded six shrill blasts. At the rail, a sailor bellowed and then flung a life ring in my direction, giving it an underhand Frisbee spin. The ring fell short, between me and the floating edge of the net, but I paddled toward it. Momentum continued to carry the ship forward, even after reversed propellers had slowed the whaler's headway. The net came, too, dragged along by the ship. As I reached the life ring, the net reached me and, with the knife in my fist forcing me to choose one or the other, I grabbed for the net with my free hand.

"All right, then!" From his perch on the float less than twenty feet away, Owen Stuart sent me a manic grin. "Have at the bugger."

As *Le Mistral*'s headway gently surfed me across the surface, I pretended to saw the net but in reality gave my attention to finding a way out of my predicament. For the moment, the cetacean biologist seemed content with his monkey wrenching, but underneath that manic exuberance I thought I detected something far more sinister. What if he had heard my gasp of surprise? What if he'd correctly interpreted the meaning of my widened eyes? What if he realized that he'd revealed himself to be Sam's killer? Each time Grandmother Massett spoke of the silver blackfish, someone died. Would I be next?

Almost by instinct, I pulled myself along the net, putting distance between myself and Sam's killer and, at the same time, moving nearer to *Le Mistral.* My gaze drifted ahead, following the curve of the net as it rose from the water and climbed toward the rail of the ship.

Climb!

My heart clonged at the thought. The rail of *Le Mistral* atop that steel cliff seemed so far away! Yet I had seen sailors on tall ships scramble up just such nets to adjust the rigging and the sails. And not long ago Jessie had coaxed me to join her on the rope spiderweb of her school playground. How hard could it be? Hand over hand, one foot after the other, and soon I'd be at the top, far beyond the reach of Owen Stuart and his awful knife. Safe!

A shiver ran through me, the first since I'd entered the water, and that decided it. If I didn't move fast, I'd lose my chance, or worse, my nerve. My dive with Dan Massett had sapped my strength, and although I'd revived some on the trip back to Hydaburg, the rough water and chill breeze combined to drain me of energy. How long could I hold out before my strength gave way and fatigue overwhelmed me?

Hand over hand, I pulled myself toward *Le Mistral.* The knife made my left hand awkward, slowing me down, so I dropped it. When I reached the spot where the net rose from the water, I looked down, not up, trying to peer through the murk so I could find a foothold. By touch more than sight, I finally managed to snag the net. Only a toe, but that was enough to lever me from the water and lift me within reach of the next rung of net.

One foot after the other, hand over hand, I inched my way up that net. Somewhere below, Owen Stuart howled with fury, but I ignored him. Somewhere above, another man shouted my name, but I ignored him, too. The breeze nudged against me, and maintaining my foothold required all of my concentration. So I looked straight ahead, focusing on the gleaming white steel of *Le Mistral*'s hull, gratified each time a neat line of rivets hove into view, wondering when I would reach the first line of portholes. Surely I'd climbed that far by now?

Then the net slipped and me with it. My feet slid off their toeholds, dangling free in the air. I slipped an arm through the net, locking the rope in the crook of my elbow, and looked up. A wide swath of net had been draped over the rail but now only a narrow thread remained. Had the net torn?

My feet bicycled, seeking another foothold. Not so far below, Owen Stuart still rode his buoy. The net had drifted along the entire length of *Le Mistral,* floating close enough to the stern to foul the propellers. Not torn—cut! To spare the ship, the whalers were cutting the net!

Far, far up the steel cliff of *Le Mistral*'s hull, Raoul D'Onofre leaned toward me over the rail, shouting urgently. "Jump clear!" He waved both hands, motioning me away from the ship. "Dive clear! Now!"

Without a foothold, how could I? But then my right foot caught. Which enabled me to snag my left foot and stand tall against the net. Slowly, deliberately, I reversed the position of one foot. Holding fast to the net above with both hands, I pivoted, putting myself face-first toward the water.

"Jump clear! Now!"

Dread weighted Raoul D'Onofre's words, and I did as he ordered, bending my knee just enough to spring off the net, off and out to soar like a bird toward the cold green water. As I flew, another bird appeared on the sea below, an eagle in blue and red that skimmed the crests of the waves like a skipping stone. And then the sea rushed up to meet me, drawing me back into her cold embrace.

Down, down, I plunged through the other-world gloom. Then the bouyant survival suit sent me back to the surface, propelling me toward the silver puddle of air above me. I burst from the water, rising above the surface to the level of my thighs, and then fell forward, landing face-first on the sodden net.

"So you are back." Owen Stuart crabbed toward me across the tangle of rope snarled on the sea's surface, the knife gleaming in his hand. "And none the worse for wear."

I dragged my feet under me and propped myself erect, trying to catch my breath. "I'm fine."

I pasted a smile on my face and glanced beyond him to *Le Mistral,* which seemed to be drifting farther away. Beyond the whaler, the rest of the mad regatta sailed on, unconcerned—unaware?—of the drama unfolding in the lee of the French ship. How long had we been in the water? Where in hell was the Coast Guard? Had that been Dan Massett's dugout heading this way?

Closer at hand, Owen Stuart still snaked his way toward me across the net, and I gave him my full attention. "I really am fine. Shouldn't you be finishing up that net?"

He dismissed my question with a snort and came on steadily.

My turn for crabbing. I scuttled backward on my rump, trying to maintain the distance between us. How much net extended behind me? Gambling that surprise might stop him, I tossed him another question. "How will you explain the knife wounds on my body?"

Stop he did, rising up on his knees for a second, as if to consider the question. Then, with a nasty grin, he allowed the knife to slip into the water and started toward me again. "Drowning will look real enough."

I glanced quickly over my shoulder to find my heading and then slid backward as fast as I could. Not much net and not much time. The plunge into the water had drained me. I played for time, hoping to surprise him again. "You nearly pulled that off once. With Sam."

My words rolled off him without braking his advance, so I tried another tack. "You're such a hypocrite, Owen. You loved that silver more than your friend. Every man has his price. What 'blood money' would you exchange for your precious whales?"

That got him. He reared up again, glaring at me across a few yards of net. "Sam left me no choice. He wanted to just leave the silver, to let the amulet dissolve into silt!" He raised a fisted hand. "But I needed the treasure to ruin Raoul D'Onofre. And it will, too." He flung out an arm to point at *Le Mistral,* which stood off a hundred yards, dead in the water. "Why do you think the whaler lays off there? By now he has heard from shore that they have found the specie in his quarters—contraband treasure from a historic wreck!"

Ever so slowly, I edged away from him. "You planted it, didn't you? That's why you were so late this morning!"

His eyes lit with triumph. "Of course I did."

Inch by inch, I crept backward. "And the amulet?"

He fingered the survival suit covering his chest, tracing the shape of the orca hidden beneath the orange neoprene. "The amulet is mine and grants to me the power of the orca, ruler of the undersea." His voice shook. "And great is his wrath!"

Groping blindly behind me, my fingers closed around seawater. I'd reached the end of the net! But Owen Stuart hadn't noticed. To keep him distracted, I lobbed more questions. "Why did you move Sam's body? And why did you kill Charley Massett?"

"To safeguard the treasure!" He sank back onto his heels, and a small frown tugged at the corner of his mouth. "If someone had found Sam in that cove, they might have started to search for the wreck. So I took him out to the strait. I did not notice the Haida fishing boat until I had rolled Sam into the sea."

He lifted clasped hands, blue eyes clouding with confusion. "So another man had to die. But compared to the survival of my orcas, what was the death of a few men?" His gaze sharpened, focusing on me. "Or the death of one woman as well?"

Too late to point out the insanity of his intention. With his greater strength, he might be able to hold my head under the water—in full view of the crewmen at the rail of *Le Mistral!* But Owen Stuart was beyond reason. In his eyes I read death—my death—and prepared to make my stand, armed only with bare hands and a full heart. His damned orcas were nothing compared to my kids. Jake and Jessie needed me, depended on me, and I would fight to the death before I'd let Owen Stuart rob them of the one parent they had left.

He crawled across the net like an orange spider on a rope web, moving slowly, deliberately. I rose into a crouch, ready to spring when he made his move. He reared up before me, gathering himself to vault forward, and a diving spear hissed past my ear to skewer the center of his chest. For an instant, Owen Stuart remained upright, a spray of blood staining his orange neoprene, and then he toppled sideways into the sea.

24

Dan Massett paddled right past Owen Stuart's body, ignoring the spear impaling his victim's chest and the sightless eyes staring at the sky, and brought his Haida dugout alongside the net. "You okay?"

I'd collapsed back onto the floating tangle of rope, legs sprawled before me and locked elbows propping the rest of me upright. "You knew he was the one. How did you know? How could you be sure?"

He rested his paddle across the gunwales of his canoe and reached behind him, lifting a crushed ammo can into view. "Remember this?"

Too tired to speak, I simply nodded. Had it only been hours since we'd found it near the Russian wreck?

He turned the can lengthwise, displaying the

letters—*OS*—painted on the side. "When I cleaned off the silt and saw those initials, I was sure enough."

Sure enough to kill a man? He'd shoved the sleeves of his sweatshirt up to his elbows, displaying the navy tattoo on his forearm. He'd been a SEAL, some kind of underwater commando, which went a long way to explaining his quick response, calculated killing and unconventional weapon. And who was I to question the man who'd saved my life? "Thanks, Dan. Without you, I'd be a goner." I tried not to look at Owen Stuart's body, floating faceup in the chop, or to let spill the tears which threatened. "I'm just sorry it had to end like this."

"Don't be." The confidence in his voice matched the certainty in his eyes. "He earned his death."

On that point, everyone seemed to agree. When Raoul D'Onofre motored up in one of *Le Mistral*'s Zodiacs a few minutes later, he spared the dead man a glance, intoned "Just desserts," and begged my pardon for cutting the net out from under me. For which crime he endured a brutal tongue-lashing from Dan Massett, who expressed outrage at the notion of sending any human being—even one zipped into a survival suit—into the cold ocean in order to prevent the fouling of his ship's propellers.

"Two more minutes, man." My partner's brown face twisted with his snarl. "In that time, she'd have been over the rail. And if you'd come to a full stop, no harm could have been done to your prop in the first place." He snorted with disgust. "Where'd you learn to sail, anyway? In a bathtub?"

While they bickered, USCG *Kodiak* steamed into view, and her captain insisted by bullhorn that all three of us—"but especially Dr. D'Onofre"—come aboard. A trio of coasties hauled Owen Stuart's body into their rescue craft while Dan Massett ferried me to the cutter. He turned over his speargun and the ammo can to the *Kodiak*'s executive officer, who led all three of us to the bridge.

Nathan Chaloner met us with a crisp salute. "Dr. D'Onofore, it is my duty to inform you that, in accordance with international law and the Marine Mammal Protection Act, the President of the United States has rescinded all permits for the taking of *Orcinus orca* in U.S. waters. You are hereby notified that the crew of *Le Mistral* immediately must cease and desist any and all hunting for protected marine mammals or face penalties including fines up to one hundred thousand dollars and one year's imprisonment."

The color drained from D'Onofre's face. "I don't understand."

Chaloner maintained his ramrod bearing but an impish light gleamed in his dark eyes. "Sir, although the commander in chief didn't share his thinking with the Coast Guard, I suspect he decided that putting a whale in a tank was just plain mean."

Winners should be magnanimous so I attempted to soften the blow. "I've never doubted that your concern for the orcas is real, Raoul. But look at the bright side—by taking this action, the President is committing the United States to preserving the species in their native habitat. Surely protecting the Earth's oceans is the best way to protect these whales."

Following the double-blow of Dan Massett's tirade and Captain Nathan Chaloner's bad news, Raoul D'Onofre beat a hasty retreat to his own ship, explaining that as the confrontation with Owen Stuart unfolded, he'd received an urgent summons from shore. "From your FBI! They are claiming that I looted a sunken treasure ship of some sort." I offered a quick explanation, assuring him that I would put in a good word with Colleen Malloy, before he climbed into *Le Mistral*'s Zodiac and motored back to his ship.

When the *Kodiak*'s executive officer led Dan Massett off for a debriefing, I stayed on the bridge to debrief the captain. "What is going on? This morning, outta nowhere, the orca hunt's on, and then just as quickly this afternoon the whole thing's off. What gives?"

Chaloner rolled his eyes and a smirk creased his dark cheeks. " 'Big government!' That's what all the talkmeisters will say. And, in this case, it's true. The secretaries of commerce and transportation signed off on the permits without checking with the White House."

He raised an eyebrow and his smirk turned into a smile of genuine warmth. "Seems the commander in chief is quite taken with your little girl. And apparently D'Onofre suspected as much. As soon as my XO delivered those permits, he put to sea. But as soon as I got the word to issue 'em, I contacted the Coast Guard's guy in the White House and asked him to double-check with the President. Took a while for him to get into the Oval Office, but as soon as he did, the President canceled those permits."

Not for the first time since I'd met him, Nathan Chaloner had stuck out his neck to do the right thing. He'd given me a head start so Sam Houston Larrabee's next of kin wouldn't learn of his death from a stranger's call. Now he'd bypassed the chain of command to take his question—and a very unwelcome question it might have been—straight to the top. "That could have been a career-killer. Making that call took a lot of guts." I offered him my hand in tribute. "On behalf of my daughter, myself and the whales, I'd like to say 'thanks a lot!'"

He took my hand and squeezed back gently. "No problem, Lauren. After all, that's what friends are for."

Friendship goes a long way to healing a hurting heart, a fact that I'd learned and relearned many more times than I cared to count. And even though I agreed with Dan Massett that Owen Stuart had earned his death, that still didn't relieve the pain of watching another human being die. Once the euphoria of my survival and rescue wore off, a deep patch of gloom infiltrated a corner of my soul and lurked inside me, ever ready to seep out and cast a pall over even my happiest moments. Sam Houston Larrabee, Charley Massett and Owen Stuart—three men had died in rapid succession and, to some degree, I had witnessed each of their deaths. Such a tally of death inevitably exacts a heavy toll. My concern for Vanessa had blunted my initial grief at Sam's loss, but in the end grieving must out, and my return to Anchorage from Hydaburg coincided with an outbreak of irritability that I couldn't seem to contain. Despite the ministrations of my kids and my housemate, I colored my days blue, blue, blue. Neither the end of Jessie's soccer season nor her decision to try volleyball in the fall succeeded in lifting my gloom. Witnessing three deaths had left a knot of misery inside me that strangled every flicker of joy.

Partly that came from worry about Vanessa, who stayed behind to finish settling Sam's affairs. Guilt gnawed me at my inability to be two places and two people at once—friend in Hydaburg and mother in Eagle River. As the weeks passed, we kept in touch via E-mail, and each message offered reassurance of her mental health, if not her efficiency. Why on earth would a woman need three weeks . . . four weeks . . . seven weeks to settle the affairs and tiny household of a single, twenty-four-year-old man? When she returned at last, pulling her red Trans Am into my driveway just before an 11 P.M. midsummer sunset, that was the first question I asked her.

She grinned at me over the low roof of her car. "Because a single thirty-eight-year-old man wouldn't get out from under my feet, that's why. And we're thinking of making him a permanent nuisance."

Vanessa and Dan Massett? The very idea robbed me of speech but not for long. "My God, Vanessa! He's so much younger!"

She rocked back on her heels and propped her hands on her hips. "Listen to you! That sounds like the social code of Attila the Hun! And who's the one with the lesbian housemate?"

A month later, she invited us all—including Jake and Jessie—back to Hydaburg for a memorial potlatch and totem raising in honor of Sam Houston Larrabee. My gloom began to lift during the feasting and gift exchange when Vanessa presented me with my own copy of *People of the Misty Isles.* Every village household—white or Haida—also received a privately printed copy of Sam's book, and many held the volumes in their hands as his totem was raised in the yard of Mission Cottage. Joe Skidegate, the man who'd displayed the button blanket at the village hall the night we'd stumbled in out of the fog, did the talking. As he explained to the assembled mourners the significance of the figures Dan Massett had carved in a log of red cedar, a lump rose in my throat. "First flies the eagle because Sam came to us in peace, a man of a different people who had love for any kind of people, for all people."

A murmur of agreement ran through the crowd, and tears spilled down my cheeks. From his spot at my side, Jake threw an arm around my shoulders as Joe Skidegate continued. "Then comes Raven because Sam heard from him who the *Haada* are and how they came to be."

On the other side of me, Jessie leaned in for a reassuring snuggle, and I managed to smile through my tears as Joe Skidegate described the final figure on Sam's totem. "Last is the blackfish because Sam became one of us when he joined our brothers in the sea."

Banishing the last of my gloom took the sea itself and a return to the Sukkwan Island cove where a shipful of Russian sailors, a great Haida chief and Sam Houston Larrabee had all lost their lives. Jake and Jessie piled out of the wheelhouse of Dan Massett's borrowed boat as soon as he dropped anchor over the spot where we'd found Sam's diving knife. They leaned over the stern, eyes shadowed from the reflecting glare by upraised hands, and tried to make out the cannons they'd heard so much about.

Jake twisted back to face me. "Mom, can't we go in? Can't we just snorkle?"

Jessie added a harmonizing whine. "Please, Mama? We can't see a thing from up here."

Dan Massett set a mesh gear bag on the deck and unzipped it. "Try one of these on for size." He held out a pair of diving masks. "Then lean over the side and stick your faces in the water—you'll see just fine."

Jake stuck out his chin. "But it's too far. I want to go down there."

"Yeah." Jessie folded her arms like a tough guy. "We want to dive!"

Oh so slowly, Dan Massett straightened himself into a military posture, shoulders wide and back straight. "We are not here for sightseeing." He lifted the orca amulet which hung from a heavy silver chain around his neck. "We are here because three men died when the silver blackfish was taken from the sea." He swept a hand from left to right, embracing the entire cove. "This is a place of death and must be treated with respect for the many men who lost their lives in these waters."

Facing him across four feet of deck, my son straightened his own shoulders and nodded. "I understand. I'm sorry, Dan."

Jessie let her hands fall to her sides. "Me, too."

And so Vanessa and I anchored my kids' legs while they leaned their faces into the water as Dan Massett hoisted bar after bar of silver specie over the side of the boat, returning the village's portion of the Russian treasure to the sea. And when the last bar had plunged to the bottom and embedded itself in the silt below, right beside the cannon my kids claimed was clearly visible with the aid of a mask, he ordered us all belowdecks. "I promised *Nani* that no one would know where the silver blackfish lies." He lifted the heavy chain from his neck. "I'll just troll around a bit, and then we'll go home."

After the silver blackfish had returned to the sea and my kids and Vanessa had returned to the wheelhouse, I stayed on deck, hanging back at the stern where the wind could whip through my hair and blow the last wisp of gloom from my soul. A ways to the north, a tiny patch of mist hung over the strait. A whale spout? I shielded my eyes with an upraised hand, searching the glittering sea for a black fin, but the dazzle off the water left me blind. As I closed my eyes against the sun's brilliance, a chorus of laughter spilled from the wheelhouse. Lifting my face to the wind and sun, I savored the warm, salty air and knew that life was good.

Author's Note

Now and then I hear from readers who would like to learn more about some of the topics Lauren Maxwell discusses in her adventures. For *Killer Whale,* I spent a lot of time sifting information about the Haida and orcas. Some useful sources include:

Barbeau, Marius. *Haida Myths Illustrated in Argillite Carvings.* Ottawa: National Museum of Canada, 1953.

Beck, Mary Giraudo. *Shamans and Kushtakas: North Coast Tales of the Supernatural.* Seattle: Alaska Northwest Books, 1991.

Blackman, Margaret B. *During My Time: Florence Edenshaw Davidson, A Haida Woman.* Seattle: University of Washington Press, 1982.

Boelscher, Marianne. *The Curtain Within: Haida Social and Mythical Discourse.* Vancouver: UBC Press, 1988.

Hand, Douglas. *Gone Whaling: A Search for Orcas in Northwest Waters.* New York: Simon and Schuster, 1994.

Kirkevold, Barbara C., and Joan S. Lockard, editors. *Behavioral Biology of Killer Whales.* New York: Alan R. Liss Inc., 1986.

Obee, Bruce, and Graeme Ellis. *Guardians of the Whales: The Quest to Study Whales in the Wild.* Anchorage: Alaska Northwest Books, 1992.